A MATTER OF EXECUTION

NICHOLAS ATWATER

OLIVIA ATWATER

1

———

THE PALE SOLDIER - THE EBON WARDEN - POORLY EXECUTED - MY DRAKE-INFESTED LONGBOAT

It was a lovely day for an execution.

The scent of lilies filled the confines of my dingy prison wagon. Chains rattled as I looked through the bars. The wagon passed through streets lined with beautiful trees; dew-speckled flowers shimmered in the sunlight that escaped through the cloudy morning sky dotted with airships. I saw reminders of the Imperium everywhere I looked—in the audacious cerulean banners that still fluttered on the breeze, and in the bold buildings of whitewashed stone. In many ways, Lyonesse remained a bastion of Imperial grace. In fact, if I hadn't known better, I never would have guessed it was a city run by petty warlords.

I couldn't have asked for a grander city in which to be executed—nor for a more perfect morning.

Faces lined the streets in growing numbers. People shouted angrily at our conveyance as it passed. Something wet and pungent thudded against the wagon's frame, spattering me with the scent of rotten fruit. There were so many furious people that, for a moment, I was relieved to be inside the wagon. The crowd surged forward, and one of the gryphons drawing my wooden prison aimed an avian hiss at the spectators, pushing them back. The teamster snapped his crop half-heartedly at the large creature, just to rein it in. Its talons click-clacked against the cobblestones—but the sound was soon lost, drowned out by the exultant fury of the gathered crowd beyond.

I wondered for an instant why the crowd was so upset with me. The militia hadn't taken the time to explain the crime that I'd supposedly committed—they'd been far too busy shoving me to the ground and screaming in my ear. But as I listened more closely to the shouting crowd, I realised that I wasn't the target of their ire.

"Murderer!"

"Justice for the warden!"

"You bloody, rotten scoundrel!"

I eyed my companion—the only other person inside the wagon, and quite possibly the most hated man in Lyonesse.

"You're the man who killed Warden Clovis?" I asked. I probably should have forced a bit more fear and a bit less curiosity into my voice, given that we were rolling along towards the gallows.

The man across from me had a mess of tangled white hair and an unkempt beard, somewhere beneath the week's worth of dirt and grime. He had strong, broad shoulders, and plenty of hard muscle; even slumped against the bars as he was, I could tell that he had a soldier's bearing. Old, layered scars stood out on his pale skin, where they weren't obscured by ragged clothing and several beatings worth of bruises.

My companion didn't respond. He stared past my shoulder with the expression of a man who was calmly preparing himself to die.

I raised my voice higher. "I *said*—"

"I heard what you said," the man replied. His voice was irritated. It was also far younger than I'd been expecting from such a greyed, beaten-down figure. He fixed hard grey eyes upon me. "Didn't think they were all here for you, did you, gob?"

The word *gob* was a slur. *Gob*, of course, is short for *goblin*—and I am a goblin. But there's something uniquely unpleasant about being reduced down to your green skin and pointed ears—as though that's all you are. Some people used the word casually, without knowing any better, and I didn't always bother to correct them. But others used it specifically to hurt. From the wrong person, in the wrong tone, the word *gob* could ruin my day.

A hanging, I reminded myself forcefully, would *end* my day. As such, I tucked my frustration beneath a pleasant smile and continued the conversation.

"Technically," I said, "none of them are here for me. I'm not the person they're looking for." I threaded my fingers together and leaned my chin atop them. "They're looking for a goblin named Besker Thews. My name is William Blair. But apparently, all goblins look alike to you people." I allowed a hint of irony into my tone.

The man across from me raised a sceptical, blood-crusted eyebrow. I rolled my eyes at him. "Five minutes from the gallows, and you've still got the time to make racist assumptions," I observed. "Bravo, sir. That's dedication."

My companion gave me a flat look. "I don't think you're a criminal because you're a goblin," he said. "I think you're a criminal because you're an Oathbreaker."

I flinched at that. It wasn't an uncommon observation— Oathbreakers don't have any visible marks, but it's easy to feel the broken Oath upon them once you get close enough. Swearing an Oath by the holy Tuath Dé is serious business. The faeries that created our world and everything in it feel very strongly about promises made in their name; breaking a vow like that leaves a permanent blemish on your soul.

It's hard to say whether people mistrust goblins or Oathbreakers more. I was both—so I rarely got the chance to find out.

I barreled onwards, determined to pretend I hadn't heard him. "I'll have you know, my airship just docked in Lyonesse yesterday morning," I said. "I'd barely been off it for half an hour before the militia decided I looked like some local nuisance of theirs."

My companion's scepticism deepened. "*Your* airship?" he asked pointedly.

I quirked a sardonic eyebrow. I'd seen that expression before. "My airship," I repeated. "People call me *Captain* William Blair, when I'm not shackled to a wagon."

The other man snorted at this. "Every man with a drake-infested longboat wants to be called *Captain* these days," he muttered.

I'd heard that sort of comment dozens of times by now—but I never *enjoyed* hearing it. I stiffened with anger, though my body was tired and sore. The man across from me clearly just wanted to continue on in silence.

He probably shouldn't have upset me, in that case. I rarely suffer in silence.

"No, please don't stop there," I said cheerfully. "Elaborate, by all means. Why *shouldn't* I be the captain of my own airship? Ah, I know —I ought to have a hat. Thankfully, I left my hat on the ship. I'm sure one of these brutes would have stolen it, otherwise." I smiled serenely at him. "I need a hat, don't I?"

The man contradicted me with a flat, steely-eyed look. "No one in their right mind would follow a—"

"—goblin?" I finished for him.

"—Oathbreaker," he corrected me, nearly at once.

"Of course," I said sardonically. "We have already established that you have a problem with… *Oathbreakers.*"

The ragged man shook his head at me. He withdrew back into himself, attempting to concentrate once again upon his impending doom.

"You're not an aethermancer, are you?" I pressed him.

He groaned and cast his eyes upwards, as though to beg the holy Tuath Dé for assistance. I felt a spike of petty satisfaction at his discomfort, though I'd asked the question for good reason.

"What?" I said. "Your eyes have lost their colour, and your hair's gone prematurely white. I bet if someone washed you clean, you'd have a few blue veins underneath that dirt. You've clearly been exposed to staggering amounts of aether. So, you're either an engineer or else you're an aethermancer. And since you somehow murdered the second-best aethermancer in this entire city, it stands to reason—"

"I am not an aethermancer," my companion growled. "Do you really think you'd still be alive and bothering me if I was?"

I nodded sagely. "Point taken," I said. "Those aren't the scars of an engineer, though. Curious." I discarded that vain hope with a sigh. An aethermancer would have been terribly helpful right now. "If I might ask you something else, Mr..."

My companion snorted at the polite form of address. "Strahl," he said. It was the closest thing to a non-answer he could have given me. Strahl had been a plentiful name, even before the war. The common strahl was a bird known for fostering other birds' abandoned chicks. The name *Strahl* was reserved mostly for orphans, bastards, and people who didn't want to give their actual name.

I nodded again, as though this was a genuine answer. "Mr Strahl," I said. "If I might ask—why did you kill Warden Clovis? Surely, you had to know you'd never get away with killing one of the four wardens of Lyonesse in his own city."

Strahl shrugged uncomfortably. "Clovis made me an offer I couldn't refuse," he said. "I refused."

Hm.

I was already fairly sure I didn't like this criminal they'd stuck me with. But I wasn't sure I could convince myself that he deserved to die. I couldn't imagine what sort of grim offer might persuade a man to throw his life away in protest.

In the interest of honesty: it didn't strictly bother me that Strahl had killed a warden. As a matter of principle, I wasn't fond of the wardens of Lyonesse. The Imperium had fragmented into several independent states since the civil war; Lyonesse had established itself as one of the smallest and wealthiest city-states, on the strength of its aethermancers and on the hoarded wealth of its refugee nobility. For all that the wardens made no pretension at continuing the empire itself, they had still situated themselves as the guardians of its living remnants. I doubted if any of the wardens truly cared about the empire's memory... but they profited handsomely from it, all the same.

They were, in short, political carrion-feeders.

I glanced through the bars behind me. We had only a block left between us and the parade square. An expansive crowd had gathered around a raised wooden platform. A sturdy, well-used gallows stood at the centre, proudly visible.

I'd assumed that the militia would concern themselves mostly with the gallows itself—but while a semi-circle of men did indeed surround the platform, there were *more* armed men guarding a building just behind the square.

It was an official-looking government structure in the classical Imperial style. Judging from their positions, the militia were far more concerned with keeping the crowd away from that building than they were concerned with keeping them away from the gallows.

I pondered this for a moment, before some instinct drew my eyes upwards. The government building had a balcony. On this broad balcony stood a tall, darkly dressed woman. I couldn't see her features very well, but she was wearing true, ink-black apparel—an expensive commodity, even in Lyonesse. She was also wearing trousers. Women in trousers weren't so uncommon on the outskirts of the former Imperium, but they were still looked down upon in stuffy, high-class Lyonesse. Between the woman's trousers, her sun-bronzed skin, and her relaxed posture, I suspected she was originally from the wild, frontier Rustlands. Plenty of people came to Lyonesse from all over— in fact, primarily, they came to apprentice themselves to the four famous houses of aethermancy within the city, each one ruled by a warden of incomparable skill and power.

Well, I amended to myself. *The wardens are... mostly incomparable, I guess.* The man in the cart with me had certainly compared himself with Warden Clovis, and he'd survived the encounter better than the warden had.

Strahl noticed the direction of my gaze. "The new Ebon Warden," he observed. "Jasmine Albright. She came to make sure they kill me properly, I guess."

I raised an eyebrow at that. "She?" I asked. "The new Ebon Warden is a woman? Well. Lyonesse has finally dipped its toes into the modern era while I wasn't looking. Good for them, I suppose. At least your death will be progressive." I tried to keep the worry out of my voice. Until this moment, I'd been fairly sure I wasn't actually going to die today. But I'd never imagined I would have to escape out from under the nose of one of the wardens of Lyonesse. I squinted at the woman's figure, searching for proof of her aethermancy. She'd pulled back her long, sable hair into a fighting braid atop her head; but were there streaks of white in there, where aether exposure had leached its colour?

"I'm surprised the wardens actually gave her the position," Strahl said dryly. "Old Drayton probably fought it tooth and nail."

"Old Drayton?" I muttered. I craned my neck, trying to get a better view of the platform.

"One of the other wardens," Strahl amended. "He's very… traditional." He twisted his mouth into a wry grimace.

Warden Albright leaned her elbows upon the balcony railing with a bored-looking posture.

Down below, a grey-clad, broad-shouldered hangman stepped onto the platform, followed by a priest of the Benefactor in his blue sash, clutching at a copy of the holy Word.

I smiled.

Strahl caught the expression. He knitted his brow at me. "What are you so happy about?" he asked.

I shrugged. "You didn't think they were all here for you, did you?" I asked him mildly.

The city militia approached the end of our wagon. One of them fished for their keys, and I felt a bolt of urgency. I had to make my decision now.

But it wasn't *really* much of a decision, was it? I somehow needed to escape the new Ebon Warden. Normally, I would have considered that to be an impossible task… but I was standing next to the very man who'd killed Warden Clovis.

"Mr Strahl," I said. "As it turns out, I am not in the mood to die today."

Strahl turned an impressively level expression upon me. "Let me know how that works out for you," he said.

"I could use your assistance," I told him. "If you were feeling in a similar mood, I mean. I am confident that I can handle every obstacle *except* for the Ebon Warden. But you've tangled with a warden already. If she becomes a problem, I'd appreciate your help."

For a moment, I thought the man might actually refuse. A heavy, jaded weariness flickered across his bruised features, and I wondered if Strahl hadn't already made his peace with the rope. But he sighed and nodded minutely. "I've got an Oath to keep," he murmured. "I may as well tell Death Victorious I gave it my best try."

"Just one minor detail," I added with a wince. "Please refrain from killing anyone. I'd prefer if we weren't chased to the furthest corners of Avalon because we left a mound of corpses behind."

"You want to escape an angry crowd, an armed militia, and a warden of Lyonesse… and all without killing anyone?" Strahl asked. His tone was incredulous—but after a moment, he chuckled. "Sounds like a challenge," he admitted. "What's the plan?"

I smiled helplessly. "No idea," I admitted. "They haven't had the chance to tell me."

The militia unlocked the door. One of them stepped into the wagon to undo the chains that kept us bound to the floor. He shoved us out onto the cobblestones, one after the other. The crowd erupted into bloodthirsty cheers.

I winced at the crowd's volume, and at the brightness of the morning sun. Goblins are sensitive to light, and the militia had taken my goggles. No one much cares if a dead man goes blind, I suppose.

It was a long walk to the gallows for what would be a much shorter fall.

We passed through the large ring of militia that surrounded the platform, keeping back the crowd. Four of the city's finest Lyonguard stood on the platform itself. The Lyonguard looked like classical statues in their scarlet-maned helmets and their polished, gleaming breastplates, with their hands resting upon the hilts of their sabres. Their silver gauntlets thrummed with a muted power that made my teeth ache, even from below the gallows. Minor aethermancers, all of them.

Warden Albright was going to be trouble enough—but truthfully, I hadn't expected the Lyonguard either. I had faith in my crew... but the unexpected scope of our opposition touched that faith with worry.

I ascended the steps in front of Strahl, counting obstacles out of the corner of my eye as best I could, despite the blinding sun. As the two of us reached the top, the priest moved forward to offer his copy of the holy Word to me. I placed my shackled hands dutifully upon it.

"Child of the Benefactor," the halcyon called out solemnly, "share with me now your burdens and be free of them, that your soul may return to Arcadia without regrets." He was a lean, dark man with skin the colour of swaying cattails. His hair was closely shorn to his skull in a way that emphasised the friendliness of his slightly rounded face; his mouth was lined with the evidence of many easy smiles. Even as I looked up at him, the halcyon smiled gently at me—as though I were coming home, instead of going to the rope.

Evie—a genuine halcyon of the Benefactor, and my ship's chaplain —could talk his way into the strangest places. *Everybody loves the Benefactor, Wil,* he liked to say. I didn't bother to question how he'd got himself assigned to this particular execution. I was just glad to see him.

A slender length of metal jabbed out from between the pages of the holy Word. I palmed the lock pick carefully.

Evie raised an eyebrow at me. "Do you have any confessions, my friend?" he prompted me again, with a hint of smirk.

I shook my head. "Maybe after breakfast," I mused.

A few people chuckled. A guard clubbed me upside the head hard enough to make me see stars. Evie caught me as I stumbled back—he turned his body to shield me from view as I struggled for the presence of mind to pick at my manacles.

"Thank you, Evie," I mumbled.

"Thank me after breakfast," Evie whispered back. He helped me back to my feet—then whirled upon the guard that had clobbered me. "This man is in his final moments!" Evie scolded sternly. "It is incumbent upon *all* of us to show him some modicum of mercy—"

I tuned out the rest of Evie's sermonising tirade to focus on my shackles. Somewhere in between *love of the Benefactor* and *duty to use that mercy with which He blessed us*, the lock gave a quiet click. When I looked up again, I saw that the guard actually looked chagrined.

One of the Lyonguard stepped forward, carrying a writ in his hand. The extra plume in his helmet and the regal sash across his chest suggested that he was slightly more important than his fellows. He reached for the small vox station nearby, grabbing the chatterbox and turning it on. The emitter squealed as he adjusted the knob, and a wince rippled through the crowd.

"People of Lyonesse," the Lyonguard addressed the crowd monotonously. "We are gathered here today to see justice done…"

I glanced sideways towards the executioner as the Lyonguard prattled on about justice, honour, and the public good. The executioner was a tall, broad-shouldered man with russet brown skin —further darkened from a life outdoors. I would have found him imposing… but a pair of warm brown eyes stared back at me from within the black executioner's hood. The executioner winked at me, and my hopes soared in reply.

Evie rarely walked into danger without his beloved husband—a man who also happened to be my best friend and first mate, Samuel "Little" Méndez.

Little held my gaze for a moment; then, he gave a short jerk of his hooded head towards the skyline. I followed his silent suggestion, searching through the ships that milled about this morning. My *Iron Rose* wasn't among them… but an old clanker had begun its approach towards our general area with a familiar single-pilot outflyer clamped beneath it. Even as I watched, the outflyer's drives ignited, and the clanker's clamps released it for flight.

I was fairly certain it was illegal to fly a fighter plane over an execution. I was equally certain that the pilot in question did not care.

The Lyonguard wound his speech to an end, oblivious to the approaching outflyer. He turned towards me, and I knew that he intended to offer me up to the unruly gathering as an appetiser before the main course.

"Any last words, goblin?" the Lyonguard sneered.

"Many, sir," I answered. "But none for polite company."

A few snickers went up among the crowd. The Lyonguard didn't even break a smile. He slashed a hand through the air, giving the signal to proceed.

Little held the noose up before me, silently judging its width against my neck. He tapped his fingers meaningfully against the knot, and I suppressed my smile. Little was a seasoned airman; he knew a thing or two about tying knots.

In this case, of course, he'd been very careful *not* to tie a knot. One good tug would probably make the whole thing come apart.

Little looped the noose around my neck. Butterflies danced in my stomach as the rough hemp scratched at my skin. I knew my best friend wouldn't strangle me... but my nerves weren't quite as convinced on the matter.

"How about you?" the Lyonguard growled at Strahl. "Any last words?"

Strahl stared at him with a stony face. I wondered if he'd decided I was playing a joke on him, until he made his reply. "I'd ask you the same," he told the Lyonguard, "but I already promised not to kill anyone today."

The Lyonguard snorted in derision.

One of the militia started up a drumbeat nearby, trying to signal the crowd to hush up. The sound didn't quiet anyone, of course, but it did set a pace for Little, who started back towards the lever that would swing free the panels beneath us.

He didn't even set his hand upon the lever before chaos erupted.

The Lyonguard in charge staggered violently back and crumpled to his knees. The crowd was shouting far too loudly for anyone to have heard the gunshot—but I knew that there had been one, nevertheless. My gunnery chief, Miss Lenore Brighton, had remarkable aim.

I might have searched the rooftops for her figure, had the gull-winged outflyer above not taken that exact opportunity to dive at the plaza. The one-manned fighter wove through the scattered air traffic above, roaring so dangerously close to the gallows that the platform rattled beneath our feet.

Crowds screamed and scattered. I screamed with them, straining against the noose as I tried to duck for cover. But the outflyer swerved just in time to avoid a fatal crash, pulling upwards into the sky once more.

Maybe I was just imagining things, but I thought I could hear Dougal MacLeod's mad, booming laughter echoing above the din.

"Daft, sky-drunk Northerner!" I gasped, as I struggled free of my manacles. "He's going to kill us all!"

One of the other Lyonguard on the platform caught sight of my struggles. He pulled his sword only halfway before Little slammed his heavy boot into the back of the Lyonguard's knee, driving him down. I slipped the noose free of my neck just as Little smashed the man's helmet into the wooden railing, ringing him like a bell.

The Lyonguard slumped into a daze. Little reached down calmly to pick up his sword. He tossed the weapon my way; I snatched it from the air, testing the weight of the unfamiliar blade. It was a quality weapon, but far too heavy for me. Still—it would have to do.

The two Lyonguard next to Strahl turned towards Little—but they'd somehow forgotten the dangerous man beside them.

Strahl burst into a flurry of motion. He slammed his elbow into the closest man's faceplate, even as his boot lashed out to crack at the other man's knee. The first guard recovered quickly enough to draw his blade. Vials of aether on his person hissed and clicked as they infused his gauntlet and traveled along the blade; the edge crackled audibly with discharged aether, hissing at the air. He turned and stabbed at the manacled man behind him… but he was far too slow.

Strahl looped the chain of his manacles over the blade with surprising alacrity; he jerked the sword wide, pulling his chains tense against its edge. Strahl's arms bulged for a long second before the aether-honed sword cut through the chain, neatly freeing his movements. He sidestepped behind the Lyonguard, slamming his shoulder into the other man's back to launch him directly into his injured, kneeling comrade.

I barely managed to follow the flurry of violence. If I'd been under any remaining illusions as to the convict's deadly skills, I was now utterly disabused of them.

Strahl shrugged himself free of his noose, as though it were an afterthought.

The two Lyonguard near Strahl struggled to rise again... but I noted their current position with detached interest. I recovered from my worried awe just long enough to step back and kick the lever.

The platform's floor swung open; two Lyonguard dropped from sight with sharp cries of shock.

Strahl shot me a brief, startled blink. He kicked a dropped blade up into his hand, though, and turned to survey the situation.

The crowd had surged away from the platform in a panicked frenzy, desperate to escape the sudden danger. The militia in front of the government building pulled backwards, tightening their semi-circle in order to protect the notable figure upon the balcony.

Crack! A bullet skipped off the wall just beside that dark figure, kicking up a cloud of dust. Miss Brighton certainly could have hit her mark if she'd been trying—which meant she was probably just aiming to distract the warden. But the wardens of Lyonesse were a far cry from the pampered nobles of yesteryear's empire.

Warden Albright didn't duck or dive for cover. Instead, the air around her shimmered with spent aether, and a low, painful humming cut through the air of the plaza. The warden leapt from the balcony in one smooth, impossible movement. Flashes of blue-white aether slowed her fall just as she would have hit the floor, settling her gracefully upon the ground at the last moment. The wavering aether around her remained, crackling into a pointed edge that scattered the crowd and her own militia before her.

She was coming straight for us.

The militia around the platform struggled free of the crowd's last fleeing stragglers and raised their guns to fire upon us. But we'd all somehow managed to forget the outflyer and its reckless pilot. The fighter craft had flipped around for *another* death-defying dive. All of us—even the dark, advancing warden—threw ourselves down to the ground as the outflyer roared past. It passed low enough to the ground this time that it kicked up plumes of dirt, leaving a haze in its wake.

Dougal MacLeod had more than thirty years of experience as a combat pilot. I tried desperately to remind myself of this fact as I crawled back onto my feet, shaking my head to clear the panic from my veins.

Another *crack!* rang out across the square—more audible this time, now that the crowd had dispersed. Miss Brighton's bullet caught against the warden's wavering shield of aether, evaporating against it in a snap of blue-white lightning. The warden was back on her feet, and her militia had rallied behind her.

As a longtime school teacher and onetime bounty hunter, Miss Lenore Brighton was nothing if not adaptable. She swiftly changed her tack.

Another *crack!* sounded. This time, one of Warden Albright's militia staggered back, clutching at his shoulder. Albright whirled, and I felt a brief pang of empathy for her. *At least she cares about her people,* I thought.

"How in rot and ruin are we getting out of here?" Strahl demanded, just next to me.

"Transportation is on the way!" I yelled back. "I'm right about that, Little, aren't I?"

My first mate couldn't hear me over the din—but that was fine. Little had been mute for years now, and we'd all learned to work around it. I shoved the heavy sword under my arm and flicked my fingers at him, conveying the same message in sign language. He nodded and signed back to me: *Buy time.*

Two of the city militia started up the back stairs of the platform, swords drawn, and Little turned his attention their way. He flipped a foot-long steel rod from his person, snapping it out into a telescopic staff with a spring-loaded *click-clack.*

Evie stepped between Little and the advancing militia, holding up his hands. "Gentlemen," he said loudly. "I'm sure this is all just a misunderstanding. Let's all lay down our arms and talk, shall we?"

One of the militia shot Evie an incredulous look. "*Move*, halcyon!" he said sharply.

"Please," Evie begged, "allow me to appeal to your better natures!"

The militiaman shook his head; he and his comrade charged, clearly intent on shoving past the naive priest.

Evie yanked the blue sash from his body and lashed out like a serpent. The heavy fabric snapped harmlessly against the advancing man's face—but it was only a distraction. Evie kicked the man's sword neatly aside, then lunged just inside his guard. He looped the sash around the man's neck in one fluid movement; then, he knelt and hauled the man over his shoulder, flinging him off the platform and onto the stones of the parade ground.

Evie pulled back quickly, holding up his sash before him with a sheepish smile. "Might I appeal to *your* better nature, sir?" he asked the second man.

"Aim!" a sharp voice barked behind us.

I turned and saw a motley firing line of militia. They weren't neatly placed—but then, they didn't need to be. They had us surrounded, with nowhere to run.

I'm not precisely a religious man... but I like to think that the Lady of Fools and I have an understanding. She has a way of laughing as I end up in the most ridiculous situations... and I have a way of madly dancing myself to safety.

My eyes landed on the vox device, just beside us. I dived for the chatterbox and yanked it from its cradle, slamming desperately on the emitter.

A shriek like a bean sidhe's wail ripped across the plaza. A wave of shots went wide, as militia flinched and clutched at their ears. Bullets slapped against the wooden platform; woodchips scattered. A bullet flew just past my nose, cracking into the vox itself—the squealing rose sharply, and then went dead.

My ears rang; my stomach heaved with nausea. But a leviathan shadow crossed over the square, blotting out the sun, and I knew that the Lady of Fools had kept our unspoken bargain.

I couldn't hear the hum of my beloved ship—but I *felt* it in my bones. It thrummed against my skin, even from a distance. Never in my life had I been so happy to see those white sails snapping against blue skies. The onetime Imperial ship-of-the-line steered slowly above us, guarded by the mad outflyer that still danced a warding circle around it. Not that the *Iron Rose* particularly needed guarding. Several of its cannons and one of the four turrets mounted on the underside of the wooden hull turned warningly upon the square.

Next to me, Strahl rose slowly to his feet. His gobsmacked expression would remain etched in my memory for years to come.

"How do you like my drake-infested longboat?" I asked him loudly.

Lines dropped towards the platform from above, dragging against the wooden planks as the ship slowly passed. I grabbed at a rope, knowing that we had a narrow window of escape.

But Little and Evie were suddenly nowhere to be seen.

A hard spike of fear coursed through me. I dropped the rope, rushing for the stairs that led off the back end of the gallows.

"Where are you going?" Strahl bellowed.

I saw the problem as I reached the top of the stairs; Evie leaned awkwardly against the platform, clutching at his leg where a stray bullet had caught him. Blood seeped through his fingers.

It was a lot of blood.

Little knelt beside his husband, looking him over with alarm. He snatched at Evie's sash, tying it around the injury. Evie protested weakly—I'm sure there's some doctrine against using holy symbols that way—but Little neatly ignored him. Still, I knew there was no way Evie would make it to a rope in time... and obviously, his husband wasn't going to leave him behind.

I certainly wasn't going to leave *without* them.

I turned and bolted for the nearest snaking rope. Strahl watched me with a rope in his own hand; his face was inscrutable, but he'd kept his grip loose enough that the rope slid slowly through his palm. I noted him distantly as I snatched at lines, rushing them back towards the stairs.

I wasn't sure how bad Evie's injury was—but we didn't have much time to inspect it. Little had tied it off as best he could. "Up we go!" I gasped out, as I passed them each a rope. Evie grabbed one from me, though his grip was weak. Little looped the line around his husband's waist, knotting it carefully.

Unfortunately, I'd somehow managed to forget about the dangerous aethermancer behind us.

The wooden planks beneath my feet blew out from under me in a blinding flash. I heard a deafening crack—and then, I was tumbling end-over-end, rolling across the stones of the square. Stars blossomed before my eyes, and it took me more than a few seconds to clear them.

Everything hurt. My ears rang. My bones hummed.

A dark figure strode through the broken gallows platform towards me. Warden Albright's black garb had bleached to a dull, dishwater grey along her arms; her eyes burned with a shifting rainbow iridescence. Lightning crackled along the bulky gauntlet on her arm, pooling into her outstretched hand.

Every Ebon Warden for the past few decades had styled themselves after Death Victorious, the Tuath Dé of glory. Warden Albright had held the position for less than a week—but she carried her mantle of office well. She stalked towards me with all the grim finality of a large, predatory cat.

It was because she had her eyes on me that she never saw Strahl coming.

He swung from the top of the broken gallows, gripping at the very same noose that should have hung him. He slammed his boot-heels into the warden's back, picking her up off her feet and driving the air from her lungs.

The two of them tumbled across the open ground—but Strahl was up on his feet in a moment, freshly bruised and bloody.

Warden Albright struggled to rise after him; aether gathered around her, and her bulky gauntlet whirred dangerously... but Strahl didn't give her the chance to expend the deadly charge. He kicked the warden brutally across the face, and the tense cloud of aether collapsed in a rush.

The entire exchange had taken only seconds.

Strahl hauled the limp warden up in front of him, just as a dozen militia trained their guns upon his form. The men on the other side of those guns hesitated, and I silently thanked the Lady of Fools once again.

I pushed up carefully to my hands and knees. Strahl backed closer towards me, keeping the warden's figure carefully interposed between himself and the militia.

"Drop the warden!" one of them yelled.

I saw Little tug on Evie's rope behind us, signaling to the crew above to start pulling him up. Strahl glanced back towards me… and I nodded quickly.

Strahl faced the militia with a grim smile. "Catch," he told them.

He tossed the Ebon Warden towards the armed men.

One of the men was just foolish enough to take a shot. Strahl flinched—but I couldn't tell where he'd been hit. Shortly thereafter, however, an answering shot cracked through the air from one of the rooftops. The militiaman who'd fired on Strahl staggered and fell to one knee, clutching at his hip.

Militia dove for cover. Strahl lunged for the nearest line, hauling himself up hand over hand. "Get that green rear into gear, Blair!" he bellowed at me.

I bolted clumsily for a rope. Bullets whizzed by me like angry bees —but somehow, I closed my fingers around the line just in time. I mumbled a litany of nonsense as the crew above began to pull me up. Some of the words were curses; others, I think, were wild prayers. But soon, I was swinging through the air just beneath my ship, laughing with manic triumph.

The *Iron Rose* picked up speed sharply, rising towards the open skies. Bullets continued zooming past me, but I was moving far too fast to be a meaningful target now. Three other figures dangled within my sight, and I breathed out a sigh of relief as I saw them.

Thankfully, many hands above made for light work. Several people hauled me over the railing in short order. I tumbled gracelessly onto the deck of my ship, trembling with demented laughter.

Cheers went up among the crew; the sound blurred together into a roar in my ears. I tried to push to my feet, but I had to half-crawl my way to Evie's side, nearby.

Little leaned his husband carefully back against the railing. It was clear that Evie had taken a bullet to the leg—but he wasn't bleeding out as terribly as I'd feared. He wouldn't be walking again anytime soon, but I was confident that our physicker could handle the damage.

Little tore away the black hood. His brown eyes showed terrible concern, but Evie squeezed his hand and shot a weak smile in my direction.

"And how was your shore leave, Wil?" he asked in a shaky voice.

I shook my head incredulously at him. "You're a fool," I informed him. I shoved to my feet and glanced around at the other faces surrounding me. "You're *all* fools," I added, pitching my voice louder for good measure. "And aren't you all a sight for sore eyes, you lovely bunch of miscreants?"

Laughter rippled across the deck. Several people shot me ironic salutes, and my heart swelled with sentiment.

"All hands, to your stations!" I called out. "Lyonesse can kiss our rudder!"

*Aye-aye*s echoed across the main deck as people rushed back to their tasks.

Strahl knelt awkwardly on the deck, clutching at his arm. Blood had begun to stain his ragged shirt—but the bleeding was sluggish enough that I knew the injury wasn't serious. Strahl watched with a mystified expression as I patted Evie on the shoulder and turned to hold out my hand.

"Mr Strahl," I said. "That was some timely help back there with Evie. I think it's safe to say we owe you a debt of gratitude."

Strahl looked at my hand—and then, he looked at the ship beneath our feet. The idea that I *truly* owned a ship seemed to stymy him even more than the gallows had done.

He regained himself, however, and reached up to clasp at my arm. He nearly unbalanced me with his weight as he hauled himself to his feet... but I did my best to pretend at dignity, all the same.

"I'm not a very good man, Captain Blair," Strahl told me seriously. "But I don't leave people behind."

It did not escape my notice that he'd used my title this time.

I nodded back at him. "Go sit with the halcyon," I said. "We'll have the physicker patch you up."

2

MY FAIR GUNNERY LADIES - FULL STEAM AHEAD - A GOOD CAPTAIN - THE NAVIGATOR

We took a short stopover at a clock tower close to the parade grounds, where a familiar longboat unmoored itself to rejoin the Iron Rose. Once the boat had docked, Miss Lenore Brighton and her young gunpowder squire, Mary, joined us on the deck.

Miss Brighton had once been a Rustlands schoolmarm, and her attire still showed it. She wore a no-nonsense dress with a high collar and a cameo at her throat; her wide-brimmed hat hid dark walnut skin and neatly coiffed, storm-cloud black hair, streaked grey by stress and middle age. Most people found my gunnery chief pleasantly attractive—until they noted the bandolier of munitions across her chest and the rifle across her back, of course.

Mary, the twelve-year-old girl next to her, was currently dressed in more masculine clothing, wearing trousers, shirt, suspenders, and a flat cap. None of us knew her exact parentage—Mary included—but her raven hair and dusky skin suggested she was mixed-race. Mary could have convincingly pretended relation to several of the other crew aboard the ship—and while she was technically related to none of us, we were all happy to claim her as family.

It was rare to see Mary without a book in her hand—but she'd made concessions to the job today. Mary was unusually serious and intense for a child her age; she'd survived off of pickpocketing and scraps before being brought aboard the *Rose*, and I often had the impression that her childhood had not been pleasant. Under Lenore's tutelage, however, Mary had acquired a love of reading—as well as the ability to strip a rifle in record time.

Mary normally carried an odd sort of dignity for a twelve-year-old; but today, she rushed across the deck and threw her arms around me while I tried to clutch at the wheel.

"Oh," I said. "Good morning, Mary."

"I was so worried, Captain," Mary mumbled into my shirt. "We all were. They didn't hurt you too bad, did they?"

I winced as she tightened her arms around my bruised ribs. "Not… too badly," I wheezed. I couldn't bring myself to shove her off, though. "We're in a hurry to leave Lyonesse though, darling. Could you be a dear and ring Mr Finch to prepare us for a minute of hard-burn?"

Mary released me instantly, and I breathed a quiet sigh of relief.

"Aye-aye!" she said, with a crisp salute. "Yessir, Captain sir!"

Mary had always loved the aesthetic trappings of ship life far more than she loved actually following orders. Her favourite novel, *The Strange Adventures of Jack Blue*, featured a dashing aethermancer pirate, and it was clear to all of us that quiet, severe Mary hoped to follow in his fictional footsteps. Today, at least, I suspected she would remember to follow my orders, since I was pathetically injured.

Mary scurried for the longhorn with unusual obedience. I looked further down the ship towards my gunnery chief.

"Impeccable shooting as usual, Miss Brighton," I observed cheerfully. "I hazard you taught those militia a *lesson* or two today."

Lenore's cool expression didn't budge—but I thought I saw a brief glimmer of appreciation in her eyes. "Cap'n," she said, "I'm inclined to be generous, as you've had a hard few days. But it's far too early in the day for puns." Lenore had a mild Rustlands accent, but her elocution was painfully on-point from years of teaching grammar.

I grinned, still feeling punch-drunk. "You love them," I accused her.

Lenore sniffed, but said nothing further.

"MacLeod is still running interference against any outflyers that might give chase," I told her. "Do you think you and the gunnery ladies could man the ship's guns so he can dock again?"

This time, Lenore gave me a vicious smile. "We can be very persuasive, Cap'n," she said.

Mary straightened with interest. "I'll man a turret," she volunteered quickly.

Lenore narrowed her eyes. "You will not," she said. "You aren't old enough, Mary."

It was a common argument aboard the ship; lately, it had started coming up at least once a day. Mary's duties as a junior gunnery lady were mainly restricted to reloading and weapon-cleaning.

Mary narrowed her eyes in a petulant expression. A voice murmured through the longhorn before she could protest, however, and she was forced to return her attention to it.

"That's right, Mr Finch," Mary said into the receiver. "Full burn, please. And yes, the captain's onboard. He said he's right as rain!" Mary paused to listen, and then heaved a disgruntled sigh. *"Really*, Mr Finch?"

She hung up the longhorn.

"Ah," I said. "Let me guess: I forgot to buy him tea again."

"Unbelievable," Mary scoffed. "You were being *hanged!*"

"I believe his exact words were *if you don't come back with tea this time, it had better be because you're dead.*" I paused. "I seem to have disappointed on both counts."

"He's so *grumpy*," Mary grumbled fiercely. "I swear, I'm going to give him a talking-to—"

"Mary," Lenore said warningly. She jerked her chin towards the stairs that led below deck. "The cap'n is busy. You can talk with him later."

Mary whirled for the stairs with a last, indignant huff. Lenore nodded at me sharply before following suit.

Little stood among the chaos on deck, whistling at the crew and flashing orders with his hands. Normally, Evie would have stood next to him, echoing his orders aloud, but he was currently busy having his leg stitched up. To be fair, Evie was a poor substitute bosun even on his best days—he had a habit of making every order sound like a polite request.

The approach of a rumbling engine to the side of the *Iron Rose* pulled my attention from the rest of the crew. Dougal MacLeod's gull-winged outflyer rose alongside us; from where I stood at the helm, I could just barely make out his head in the cockpit. I flicked the longhorn's switch, just next to me, and the device crackled obligingly.

"Damn'd good tae have ye back, lad," Dougal's cheerful voice boomed through the connection. *"Had a good shore leave?"*

I didn't have the heart to tell him someone else had beaten him to the joke. "Lyonesse is a lovely city," I replied instead, "but I wouldn't want to hang around there indefinitely."

If Lenore had still been there, she might well have shot me for the pun.

Dougal guffawed over the channel, as the outflyer banked aside and picked up speed. *"Ah'll keep an eye out and make sure we dinnae pick up a tail,"* he told me.

"Negative," I replied. "Dock with the *Rose*. The gunnery ladies are taking over. We're going to use the clouds for cover—if we did pick up a tail, we'll lose them there."

"We'll be flyin' blind in there," Dougal said sceptically.

"Nothing we haven't risked before," I replied. "It's a better option than getting into a firefight right over the city."

"Solid copy," Dougal said. I heard the agreement in his voice this time; many of the crew on the *Rose* had lived through the civil war. None of us had much of a stomach left for collateral damage. A moment later, I heard Dougal say, more quietly: *"They hurt ye, lad?"*

"I've been worse," I reassured him.

"We've aw been worse," Dougal said. *"Go see the ol' sawbones. He's been worried sick about ye."*

I sighed. "He's busy at the moment," I said. "But I'll talk to him once we've reached cloud cover."

As the *Rose*'s engines keened with powered aether, a glimmer of blue light sparkled in the air off the bowsprit. The shimmer intensified as our wind-shield manifested. The wind behind us caught the sails, snapping them to their full splendour.

Dougal's outflyer dipped beneath the *Rose*'s hull as the clouds loomed before us in a tidal wave of a wall. The longhorn squawked, and I heard Mr Finch's prim, nasal voice crackle over it.

"*Engineering reporting,*" Mr Finch declared. "*Full burn on your mark, Captain.*"

"Roger that, engineering," I called out. "You have permission to go full burn once MacLeod reports in."

"*Aye aye, Captain Blair,*" Mr Finch sniffed daintily.

I hazarded one last look over my shoulder to the shrinking, pristine cityscape below. The skies above it were abuzz with air traffic, and the distant specks of scrambling outflyers angled towards us in vain. With a sigh, I added another city to the growing list of *Nice Places We Aren't Allowed To Go.*

The *Rose* shuddered as Dougal's outflyer berthed with the ship. The heavy clamps below us latched onto the fighter with a muted *clunk.* Soon, Dougal's voice filtered over the longhorn.

"*MacLeod on board, Cap'n Blair, sir!*" the Northerner confirmed.

I squared my shoulders, gripped the wheel, and steadied my stance. A warning klaxon blared, informing the crew of our incoming burst of speed. Crew steadied themselves, clinging to rigging where they could. The engine coughed, and I dug in my heels.

The deck rattled. The sound of the ship's drives rose in pitch. Finally, a throaty roar ripped through the air.

The *Rose* launched forward with a sharp kick, leaving a trail of wispy aether in its wake. We lanced towards a mountainous wall of fluffy cloud. Though I did not count the seconds, I trusted that my meticulous chief engineer would cut the drives in *precisely* one minute. Mr Finch was as reliable as clockwork.

The drives soon went silent, leaving us propelled by our momentum and the wind itself.

The only sounds in that silence were the creaking of the rigging, the flapping of sails, and the murmurs of my crew. Cool fog closed around us in a strange dreamscape. Small beads of water condensed on my skin, and I shuddered at the chill. In all of the excitement, I had forgotten about my aching bruises. Those bruises now reintroduced themselves to me, chastising me for my rudeness.

Little's broad-shouldered figure manifested out of the fog before me, and I breathed a sigh of relief. I was far more exhausted than I'd realised.

Go see Holloway, Little signed at me. *I'll have someone handle the wheel.*

I nodded gratefully. As I pried myself free of the wheel and locked it into place, I noticed that my hand had begun to itch like nobody's business.

"The deck is yours, Mr Little," I said.

Little whistled sharply, summoning one of the crew to his side. I clapped my hand on his upper arm as I strode past him, giving it an affectionate squeeze. Little nodded, patting me gently on the shoulder in return.

As I descended the steps, I lifted my itching hand—and nearly lost my footing. Short, jagged splinters of wood stuck out from the back of it. I'd probably acquired the injury when the warden had blasted the stairs out from under me at the gallows.

"Oh," I said with a blink. "Holloway is *not* going to like that."

* * *

Holloway did not like my injury one bit.

I bore both his disapproval and my own pain with great stoicism, of course. A good captain is, after all, unflappable.

"Son of a—!"

I cut myself off abruptly, stomping my foot on the deck as Physicker Holloway yanked a splinter neatly from my hand.

I'm a *decent* captain.

"Almost done," Holloway rumbled patiently. He plucked another splinter out, and I clenched my teeth. A strangled noise escaped me; slowly, it transformed into manic, muffled laughter.

I'm *a* captain.

Holloway towered before me, gripping my wrist with one enormous hand. He used the other hand to clean my wound with a clear, violently powerful liquid. I hissed and writhed like a cat plunged into a tub of water. But no amount of struggle would free me from the casual strength of his vice-like grip.

"Easy does it, Captain," Holloway said calmly. He lifted my hand again, peering at it through the monocle that covered his one functional eye.

Physicker Holloway was getting older these days, but he was still a fighting man's sawbones. He was a square-jawed man of impressive physique, with broader shoulders than even Little. Holloway probably had enough strength in him to snap a man in two… but that had never been his way. It was the thing I most admired about him: despite that frightening strength, Horace Halbard Holloway preferred putting people back together.

A decade and a half previously, Holloway had served the Avalon Imperium as a physicker. Though the Sundering War was long over, the hobgoblin still maintained his appearance in accordance with the Imperial Navy's impeccable standards. Holloway had since traded in his naval physicker's uniform for civilian garb, but he still kept his waistcoat neat and his pale neckcloth tucked in. The short tusks that jutted upwards from his mouth were always filed and polished. He had, I suppose, developed a slight paunch in the intervening years— but I knew that there were still scars and faded sailor's ink beneath his shirtsleeves. A particularly long scar cut across the olive green skin of his cheek, running all the way down to his clean-shaven jaw. Other people probably found the scar intimidating… but I only found it familiar.

Holloway waited patiently as I finished my undignified fit. His large hand released my wrist, and he turned away to fetch the bandages.

"How's Evie?" I asked, in a strained voice. I tried to ignore the throbbing in my hand.

"The lad hasn't got much meat on his bones," Holloway rumbled. "He's lucky the bullet didn't hit anything important." He started bandaging my hand. "I pulled the bullet. He'll need rest, but it's looking positive."

"And our guest?" I asked.

"I believe he's shaving," Holloway replied distractedly. "I loaned him my kit. I stitched him up as best I could, but I'm afraid I can't do much for his ribs except advise him to rest. Same for the bruises. Still... he's tough as nails, that one." Holloway paused. His eye flickered up to look directly at me. "Is he an aethermancer?"

I shook my head. "No," I answered. "Or at least... he *told* me he wasn't an aethermancer. Frankly, if he was, I'd have expected him to use some of the ambient aether down there." I frowned. "He's an impressive fighter... but I still can't think how he managed to best Warden Clovis. Maybe he caught him by surprise?"

"Plenty of powerful men have been laid low by surprise," Holloway rumbled thoughtfully. He didn't have to elaborate; we both knew how the Avalon Imperium had ended. We'd had a front row seat to the devastation caused when the emperor's own flagship crew had turned on him.

A single moment of surprise had ended the most powerful man in the empire. Warden Clovis was a small man, by comparison.

Heavy boots stomped down the corridor towards us. The clinic's door opened with sudden force, as Dougal MacLeod made his way inside.

Even at close to sixty years of age, Dougal cut a rakish figure. Streaks of white coloured his braided, rusty red hair and beard. Like most Northerners of the high mountains, Dougal stood almost seven feet in height. He sported a beaten leather aviator's coat, with a pale Coalition ace's scarf draped across his neck and a pair of goggles resting on his chest. Laugh lines mixed freely with deep gouges of sorrow upon his weathered face.

Dougal moved to sweep me up into one of his bone-crushing hugs —but Holloway shot him a warning look and tapped his own hand demonstratively, in the same place where I had my injury. Dougal paused awkwardly in front of me at the last minute and ruffled my hair instead.

It is very difficult to glower intimidatingly at someone several times your size who has ruffled your hair. But, by the Lady of Fools, I tried.

Dougal answered my glare with a booming laugh. "There's the man ae the hour!" he declared.

"It's good to see you too, MacLeod," I said dryly. We both knew I took great comfort in his presence, in spite of my tone. "Though I think you took a few years off my life with that flying in the square."

Dougal grinned, unrepentant. "Did ye see the warden dive fae cover?" he asked. "Priceless."

"I didn't see much of anything," I replied. "I was *also* diving for cover." I pushed myself to my feet with a pained wince. "In any case—we'll need a new destination now that Lyonesse is burned for us. I'm open to suggestions."

Holloway's face took on a thoughtful expression as he turned to clean up the clinic. Dougal stroked his elegantly knotted beard, considering.

"Could always double back northward," Dougal offered. "You know the Clanhomes are always achin' fer supplies."

I chewed on the idea. Evie, Little, and I had spent our teen years growing up in the Clanhomes with Dougal. The relationship had been a fraught one, given our time as child soldiers in the Imperium, but I still had fond memories of New Pelaeia.

"You know I wouldn't mind a run northward," I said slowly. "But our coffers need something that pays well. Our repairs last month were very costly."

Holloway glanced my way. "The Emerald Spires is near enough," he said gently. "They always have a few contracts on offer. And we know they can pay." His expression said that he knew he was treading on eggshells with the suggestion.

At the mention of the Emerald Spires, Dougal made a loud hacking sound, as though he was about to spit—but Holloway shot him a flat look. "Don't. You. Dare," he said firmly. "Not in the clinic."

Dougal snapped his mouth shut and swallowed reluctantly.

"Ah'd sooner run guns tae Carrain than take blood money fae they

Spire bastards," Dougal muttered darkly. I didn't blame him; the Emerald Spires had helped lay waste to the Clanhomes almost fifteen years ago, during the Sundering War. I'd grown up in the shadow of their handiwork, looking up at the bombed-out ruins of Old Pelaeia every day.

"We could lie low in the Rust for a spell," Holloway said, breaking through the sudden silence. "Bolton always needs good smugglers, you said."

I grimaced. "Bolton always needs good smugglers because she's running goods through the Sirocco Isles," I told him. "It's lucrative work because it's dangerous. We'd either need an iron hull or a phenomenal navigator."

Holloway opened his mouth, and I knew he was about to reassure me that I was an *excellent* navigator. I cut him off ruefully. "I'm good," I said. "I'm not *that* good."

The door to the clinic opened again, and a man entered. It took a long second for me to recognise him as Mr Strahl.

He was a changed man, with his unnaturally pale hair and beard so completely shaved off. Bright blue aether-dyed veins stood out upon his hands and neck—an unnatural colour that instantly drew the eye. Strahl's white brows and dour expression still made him seem old, but his smooth skin placed him somewhere in his middling thirties, only a few years older than me. He'd been hiding an old scar beneath the ragged hair on his face—it ran across his cheek and his nose, adding to the hint of uneasy danger that he carried. His square jaw currently set off a faint frown.

"The sign on the door said the physicker was in," Strahl said. He looked briefly between the gathered men, before holding up the rolled leather shaving kit. "Thank you for letting me borrow this."

Holloway gave the man a small smile, flashing short, filed-down tusks. "It was the least I could do," he said. "A good shave goes a long way."

Strahl gave the physicker a faintly puzzled look, as though something about the conversation didn't fit. I suspected I knew what it was. The Imperial military had a habit of conscripting hobgoblins into frontline positions, believing that their greater size made them stronger and more resilient than the average human. This tendency had given hobgoblins as a whole a reputation for obedient violence. Hard men like Strahl expected hobgoblins to cause injuries, and not to stitch them up.

My own personal experiences had convinced me that hobgoblins weren't actually any more or less violent than the average human being, however. Holloway was one of the most gentle men I'd ever met—in fact, he had a penchant for writing poetry, though he was normally far too self-conscious to share it with the rest of us.

Strahl's attention now settled on the golden Coalition kerchief around Dougal's neck, though, and I saw his expression chill.

Unfortunately, Dougal caught the look. "Problem, lad?" the old ace asked calmly. He crossed his heavy arms over his chest. I felt the sudden tension in the air between them.

Strahl eyed him for a long moment. "...only if you make it one," he replied finally.

"No," I interrupted sternly, with a hint of irritation. I strode boldly between them, keenly aware that either one of them could use me as a toothpick. "I am nipping this in the bud. Now. I am not fond of problems on my ship, so there will be no problems." I glanced at Strahl. "Maybe you served the Imperium during the war. Wouldn't shock me if you did. But if you want to sing the emperor's praises and pine for the good old days, then you're on the wrong boat. If you're on my ship, then you believe the Imperium deserved to fall. If you can't abide that, you can get off at our next destination and forget we ever met."

Strahl shot me a surprised look. "You're not a Loyalist?" he asked. "I thought you served in the Imperial Navy." I didn't bother asking how he knew—people in the military had a hundred different subtle tells.

I set my jaw. "I saw Pelaeia," I told him.

It was the only explanation necessary. Strahl shifted his eyes away from me in discomfort.

"I'm glad the Imperium is gone," Strahl said softly. "Most days, I'm the first to say it. Old habits die hard sometimes, is all."

The sentiment surprised me. In the same way that Strahl had pegged me for an Imperial airman, I knew he'd been a career soldier. I'd assumed, based on his looks and manner, that he was the sort who still longed for the glory days.

"The rest doesn't matter, then," I told him. "Some of the people on this ship have made some damn fool mistakes. We're all still kicking, though, and we've got to live our lives somehow. As long as you can follow orders and you don't start waxing poetic about the Imperium, you can stay."

Dougal raised his eyebrows at me. "Yer invitin' him ontae the crew?" he asked incredulously.

I shrugged. "Doesn't strike me that he's got anywhere else to go," I said. "He's handy in a fight, and he came back to help with Evie. He didn't have to." I levelled my gaze at Strahl. "You've got a place if you want it. You've earned that much. Otherwise, you've got room and board until we reach the next port."

Strahl looked me over with a stony expression. If he felt anything in particular about the invitation, I couldn't see it on his face.

Finally, he said: "The sooner you can drop me off, the better."

Dougal scoffed, as though he'd been expecting the words.

"I need to go back to Lyonesse," Strahl added.

That earned a stunned moment of silence from all three of us.

"Back," Holloway said slowly. "To Lyonesse."

"Yessir," Strahl confirmed.

"Where they just tried to hang us," I said.

"And here I thought they were fitting me for a cravat," Strahl said dryly.

I laughed in spite of myself. I can't help but appreciate sarcasm under pressure. Dougal and Holloway didn't join me.

I shook my head and rallied my thoughts. "Why, pray tell, would you want to go *back?*" I pressed him. "There's going to be an impressive bounty on us soon. You'd be waltzing right back into the hydra's den."

Strahl's stoic face cracked with hesitation. Fear flickered in his cold eyes.

"Warden Albright has someone captive at her estate," he said. "I'm going back."

I shut my mouth at that. The words shouldn't have surprised me. Strahl's previous sentiment trickled back to mind: *I'm not a very good man*, he'd said, *but I don't leave people behind.*

"Wil," Dougal said warningly. "I know that look."

I blinked. I hadn't realised that my expression had changed. "Er— what look?" I asked quickly.

Dougal waggled a finger at me. "*That* one," he said emphatically. "The one oan yer face right this bloody second. Ye wear yer heart oan yer sleeve, an' right now it's bleedin' aw over the physick's nice, clean flair. We got 'nough trouble as is without borrowin' *this* one's an aw."

"It wouldn't be the first time," I said defensively. "We've helped out new crew before—"

"You're offering to help?" Strahl asked. For the first time, I saw clear emotion on his face. Shock was predominant there… but just beneath it was a desperate, reluctant shred of hope.

"With all due respect," Holloway interjected, cleaning his monocle, "drawing the ire of the wardens of Lyonesse is not something that we should do lightly." He paused pointedly and then looked up at me. "More than we *already* have, that is."

"On that, we agree," I sighed. I looked back at Strahl with a wince. "I might be a Fool's fool, but even I have to admit going back to Lyonesse is incredibly dangerous. And my crew still needs to make ends meet. Forgive the mercenary question, but… do you have any way to pay us? Anything of value would work—anything at all."

"I'll join your crew," Strahl replied without hesitation. "For as long as you like. And if you free Syrene, she'll join too."

"Oh, great," Dougal scoffed. He threw up his hands. "We'll have the privilege of feedin' you an' yer friend forever. Great deal."

I cast a flat look at Dougal over my shoulder. The bearded man grumbled, but he relaxed his shoulders in acknowledgement of my silent request. I didn't often ask Dougal for much, given our history, but I hate kicking people when they're down—and Strahl was clearly at rock bottom.

"And what could your friend Syrene do for us aboard the *Rose?*" I asked Strahl patiently.

"She's a navigator, sir," Strahl replied. "Best one I've ever seen."

Dougal broke his silence with another scoff—softer this time, at least. "What's a grunt like you know 'bout navigatin'?" he asked.

"Syrene's flown Rust to Rift without so much as a map or a compass," Strahl replied. "She can find fair wind in the foulest weather. She's run blockades using cloud cover—though I'm *sure* your fine crew never needs to evade the authorities." A ghost of a smirk tugged at his lips. "She even took us through El'Ramora without alerting the harpies."

Dougal straightened slightly at this. "And how'd she manage that?" he asked sceptically.

"She flew us at night, while they were sleeping," Strahl told him.

Dougal lifted a finger, as though he'd caught Strahl in a lie. "Th'aether fae the engines would've woken 'em up!" he said.

Strahl smiled grimly. "We flew on float and sail alone," he said. "You don't know her. If you met her, you'd understand. There's not another navigator like Syrene in all of Avalon. I'd swear it to Noble Gallant."

Dougal kept an incredulous expression... but I frowned thoughtfully.

"You're not Oathbroken," I said. "It didn't occur to me until now. You served in the military—I thought all of us broke our Oaths by definition when the Imperium fell."

Strahl's smile died at that. He shifted on his feet. "I swore a different Oath than most," he said. "My honour is intact. But my past isn't up for discussion."

I nodded slowly. I had made a rule of never prying too deeply into the past of my crew. Today seemed a poor day to break that rule. "I don't like making people swear petty Oaths," I said. "I believe you when you say you've got an ace navigator up your sleeve." I eyed Strahl carefully. "Are you familiar with the Sirocco Isles, Mr Strahl?"

"Can't say I am," Strahl replied. "Why?"

"We've got the opportunity to make bank with an old friend," I explained, "but we'd have to navigate the Sirocco Isles. They're full of erratic sandstorms; hurricane winds; shattered skylands with enough debris to rip the *Rose* to ribbons." I paused. "Could Syrene fly us through all of that safely?"

"Yes," Strahl said simply. "If anyone else has flown it, she can do it twice as easily."

I'd rarely heard such unflagging confidence before. Even Dougal seemed taken in now; I saw him leaning in slightly, with an avaricious look on his face. I realised belatedly that Dougal's interest was probably more in the woman than it was in the opportunity—as a skilled pilot, he'd almost certainly want to talk shop with such a legendary figure.

"...and she'll join our crew," I said finally. "For as long as I like, you said."

"Where I go, Syrene goes," Strahl said grimly. "And as you've noticed... I've got nowhere else to go. I was a dead man walking, even before the gallows. It's all the same to me where I rest my head, Captain."

I let out a breath. The statement was both reassuring and troublesome, all at once. Deadly swordsmen and uncanny navigators didn't pop up out of the ground fully-formed. Strahl's strange military Oath and his boon companion Syrene were both signs that his past *was* the sort of thing that could bite us in the rudder.

I have been called many things in my time. Some of the better things have included: Clever. Witty. Soft-hearted. Once, I had a woman call me *relatively handsome, if you don't mind green skin.* I wasn't quite so fond of that one, but she seemed to believe it was a compliment.

Either way, I've never been accused of being *careful.*

I offered out my hand. "We spring Syrene for you," I said. "In return, the both of you join this crew until I say otherwise. You'll get food and board and your rightful fair share from our jobs." I paused. "I won't make you stay forever. I like to think you'll *want* to stay, given time."

Strahl reached out to clasp my arm in a soldier's grip. Grim hope kindled behind his eyes.

"I don't want much of anything anymore, Captain," Strahl told me. "But I'll follow orders."

I shrugged and released his hand. "Then it's settled," I said. "Let's go find some volunteers."

Strahl frowned at that. "I can't imagine anyone would *volunteer* to sneak into Warden Albright's estate," he said doubtfully.

I laughed at that. This time, even Dougal gave a chuckle.

"Oh, my dear Mr Strahl," I said. I smiled and clapped him on the back. "Let me introduce you to the rest of the crew."

3

A LADY NEEDS NO INVITATION - NO SILVERWARE - PINE WHAT? - THE WARDENS OF LYONESSE

"I can't believe you talked me into this," Strahl grumbled. His voice was muffled behind the armour we'd cobbled together for him from the odds and ends in the *Rose*'s armoury. "This is a terrible plan."

"Nonsense, my good man," I said, beaming at him. "They'll never expect us to come in through the front door." I adjusted the neckcloth of my stiff servant's uniform. At five and a half feet tall—a bit taller than most goblins, but shorter than most humans—I'd had to heavily alter a human footman's old clothing to suit my height. I like to think I cleaned up well, in spite of that. Lenore had once called me *rakish*, even—though, now that I think about it, the word probably hadn't been meant as a compliment.

"Why aren't *you* wearing any armour?" Strahl asked me. "The Ebon Warden saw you just as clearly as she saw me."

I rolled my eyes. "I'm a goblin, Mr Strahl," I said. "People only ever look at what I'm wearing. Tonight, I'm dressed like a servant. I'd be shocked if the Ebon Warden gave me so much as a second glance."

Strahl didn't contradict me.

"It's still a terrible plan," he muttered.

Three days ago, we'd returned to Lyonesse as paid passengers on a small trading ship. With us, we had brought a key figure in our overall plan: the most devious and most esteemed among my gunnery ladies.

"Pray tell, what would *your* plan be, Mr Strahl?" Lady Navi asked archly. "Did you intend to hack your way into the Ebon Warden's estate?"

Jahnavi Varma was actually a noble kumari from the province of Aarushi, but people on the *Rose* had given her the affectionate nickname *Lady Navi*. Navi was always an elegant figure—but today, she was the picture of aristocratic matriarchy. The aging noblewoman had gone digging through her chests for her old jewellery and her best cerulean sari. The bright colours made for a striking effect against her tawny skin and her august, silver-threaded black hair.

Few would have guessed from looking at Navi that she had retired herself aboard my scandalous vessel and joined Miss Brighton's ferocious knitting circle of gunnery ladies. Lady Navi had accumulated over sixty years of political cunning in her time as a kumari… but her heart had always belonged to the skies.

Navi's genuine identity had granted us a few audiences with the local nobility, who always enjoyed a chance to indulge in nostalgia. Just as Navi had suspected, Warden Albright had been forced by tradition to arrange the current party—a solemn acknowledgement of the previous Ebon Warden, and of the new warden's own political intentions going forward.

None of Lady Navi's new acquaintances had been important enough to procure her an invitation to said party… but that had never stopped her before.

I had chuckled casually at Navi's jab—but my laughter withered as Strahl stayed conspicuously silent, shifting on his feet.

"Please tell me you weren't going to hack your way into the Ebon Warden's estate," I said incredulously.

"Fine," Strahl replied with a shrug. "I won't tell you that."

"I could come up with a better plan than that in five minutes," Mary observed distantly. She had *The Strange Adventures of Jack Blue* open in her hand once again. Somehow, Mary looped her hand daintily through Lady Navi's arm without looking away from the book in front of her. Navi smiled warmly, patting Mary's lace-gloved fingers.

Mary wore a particularly striking floral-patterned gown which looked suspiciously like the curtains that had disappeared from my cabin once upon a time. Someone had used makeup to subtly change the emphasis of her eyes and cheekbones in such a way that she now looked even more like Lady Navi's not-so-distant kin, sporting her best attempt at local dress.

"But why am *I* here, Captain?" Mr Finch fretted. He smoothed his waistcoat for the hundredth time since we'd arrived on the wide berth of the longboat pier. Unlike the ladies, Mr Finch currently sported *exactly* the same attire he normally wore about the engine room. I had yet to discover just how he managed to keep his formal clothing so impeccable; it was, perhaps, the last unsolved mystery aboard my boat. Mr Finch's ever-present cream overcoat complimented his dark eyes and sepia skin, drawing extra attention to the streaks of aether-bleached silver in his pitch-black hair. I knew intellectually that he was somewhere in his forties—but his early silver hair and his continually pinched expression made him look like a man well past fifty.

"You don't want to accompany me?" Lady Navi asked Mr Finch worriedly. "Oh, I'm awful. I'm so sorry for putting you on the spot, dear. I was just thinking that it would be nice for you to get out of your engine room for a change, and... and I have missed your conversation *terribly*, you know."

Mr Finch flinched. "Awful?" he repeated, aghast. "No, not at all, I... you see, it's just that... well, I *do* appreciate the sentiment..."

"Captain," Navi said to me, "perhaps it's best that Mr Finch return to the ship. I shouldn't have presumed so much of him."

Mr Finch blinked. "No!" he said hastily. "Oh my word, of course not! Captain, I assure you, that won't be necessary. Please accept my humblest apologies, Kumari—"

"—we shall simply have to manage without him," Navi sighed, ignoring Finch's protests. Her tragic tone now began to wax overtly teasing. "Dangerous as it may be."

"Come now!" Mr Finch said. "I would never send you into danger alone when you have asked for my help, Kumari."

Navi smiled and reached up to pat Mr Finch upon the cheek. "Of course you wouldn't, dear," she replied. "You're a true gentleman."

Silence fell between them.

"I hate how you do that," Mr Finch mumbled. "It's truly uncanny."

Navi smirked at him. "Oh, stop worrying so much, Walther," she said. "I promise to protect you from all of the frightening noble ladies. Truly, you're more wound up than a pocket watch. We'll have to get you a glass of wine once we're inside."

Strahl leaned towards me with a small sound of approval. "She's pretty good," he murmured.

Navi flicked her eyes towards him with a vicious little grin. She arched an eyebrow and snapped out her fan in a deadly stance that reminded me of Strahl with a blade.

"No, dear," she corrected, with imperious grace. "I'm the *best*. Now keep a sharp eye, young man; you might learn something."

Strahl's helmeted head rocked back. "Yes, ma'am," he replied, amused.

Lady Navi was already striding forward, however, such that the rest of us had to hurry to keep up with her.

The masoned pier had several staircases leading down to the main road below. Aether-powered lamps lined the street on poles, casting their ghostly light through the golden globes that encased them. They swayed gently in the dying light of the day, casting a warm and inviting glow upon the path that led to the Ebon Warden's chateau.

We caught up with Navi at a set of iron gates, blocking off the chateau. Flanking the gates were two marble columns, carved to resemble towering mechanical suits of armour. I shivered at the sight. They were clearly meant to look like wargears—another legendary remnant of an empire better left dead. Once, I would have killed just to catch a glimpse of a real wargear and its pilot. Since seeing Pelaeia, I'd begun to hope the monstrous living machines were all on a scrap heap somewhere.

Just past the gate, I could make out the Ebon Warden's newly-inherited chateau. It was a high-vaulted building, set with impressive stained glass windows that currently glowed from within. The chateau was a work of art, built to impress and not to protect. Lyonesse was safe because of its aethermancers, and not because of its architecture.

Other elegant longboats and airborne carriages docked nearby, carrying their esteemed noble charges. A small flood of Lyonesse's rich and powerful flowed like a river towards the main gates of the warden's estate, brandishing invitations at the liveried staff. Navi strolled proudly forward, though she leaned at times upon Mary, implying enough age that she required the young girl's strength to keep her upright. I followed very closely behind them, casting my gaze low so as to avoid eye contact.

We halted at a short podium which currently blocked the open gates. A majordomo in a powdered wig fixed Navi with a polite smile, holding his hand out for her invitation.

We didn't have one, of course.

Navi smiled coolly back at him, unmoving. The two waited in increasingly awkward silence, until the servant finally cleared his throat and spoke.

"Er," he said, with forced warmth in his tone. "Good evening, my lady. Might I have your invitation?"

"My invitation?" Navi asked sweetly. "I was told there would be one waiting for me, dear."

From anyone else, this might have been a transparent gambit—but Navi was so obviously a venerable lady of means that her response immediately flustered the majordomo. I saw him check the podium in front of him, as though an extra invitation might suddenly appear upon it.

"I'm visiting, dear," Navi added helpfully. "Lady Chartrands said she would take care of putting me on the list." Her face took on a fond expression. "Why, the last time I saw Lyonesse was probably before you were born! I remember it from before all of this nonsense with the wardens. It was most famous for its chocolate then. Its chocolate!

Can you imagine? I decided to stop over on my way to Caliban's Wall, just to take a nibble—"

The majordomo stared at Navi with the helpless horror of the hired help as she prattled on, clearly forgetting the subject at hand. He tried here and there to put a word in edgeways, to steer the conversation back to the matter of the invitation she did not have. Behind us, the line of notables steadily grew.

"My lady—" he tried desperately. "Er, please, er—your name, madam? I'm sure you're on the list, if you'll just let me check."

Navi blinked dazedly. "My name?" she asked. "Oh, silly me, I forgot I wasn't at home! I'm so used to the servants knowing everything from my tea to my shoe size!" She glanced fondly back at me. "You know how I take my tea, don't you, William?"

The majordomo looked at me pleadingly, and I suppressed a smile. "Kumari Jahnavi Varma," I told him helpfully.

The poor man nodded at me, flipping through his list. His momentary relief soon turned to exasperation, though, as he failed to find the name in question.

"That's *Jahnavi* and not *Jahnvi*," Navi added, with a dim sort of smile. "Lady Chartrands certainly knows better, but perhaps one of the servants heard her incorrectly. I suppose you'll need to check for both names."

The majordomo pored frantically over his ledger. Once. Twice. I pitied him just a little bit, knowing that an extra letter would hardly make the difference.

"Young man?" Navi asked patiently. "Might we please go inside? I'm beginning to catch a chill."

The majordomo smiled nervously. "I'm afraid I do not have your name here, my lady," he admitted awkwardly. Someone behind us cleared their throat in annoyance, and he waved the next couple hastily forward, taking their invitation and letting them inside as he tried to balance his attention towards Navi.

All pleasantness left Navi's face in a moment. Her manner turned frosty. "Pardon?" she asked.

She enunciated the word so clearly that it carried above the din of the other conversations behind us. That word hit the majordomo like a bullet. I saw him squirm in expectation of the difficulties he knew to be just ahead.

"What *have* you all done with this city?" Navi demanded. "First, there were those outrageous docking fees—essentially robbery, you know, we paid a *tenth* of those in my day—and then, the absolute dearth of proper dressmakers—"

The majordomo twitched, and I knew he had barely stopped himself from pressing a hand to his face.

"—my tea was *bitter*, and you know, it's the only pleasure I have left in my old age—"

Impatient, scandalised whispers had begun in the crowd behind us. I turned around to scan the faces there as Navi continued her tirade, searching for familiar attendees. I caught sight of the very people I was hoping to see: a husband and wife with whom Navi had supped only yesterday in order to set up our current deception.

I turned back towards Navi and gave her the cue we'd agreed upon. "Would Her Ladyship like me to secure a carriage back to the city?" I offered meekly.

Navi whirled upon me in a huff. I pointed helpfully—not at the pier, but at the familiar couple just behind us. Navi locked eyes with the husband and wife, feigning surprise and fleeting recognition as they broke away from the crowd to speak with her.

"My Lord and Lady Fortinault," Lady Navi greeted them—now a woefully upset, aging lady rather than a scathing noblewoman. Mary joined in on the act, sniffling lightly. Her eyes shimmered with unspent tears that made her look even younger than her actual age.

"Kumari Varma!" Lady Fortinault greeted her, obviously concerned. "What on earth is wrong?"

"You remember that Lady Chartrands was supposed to secure us an invitation?" Lady Navi lied woefully. "Perhaps it's been lost. Or, oh —perhaps she *forgot*. How humiliating." Her tone bordered on tears. "I feel like such a fool. Look at me: turned away like some vagrant. My poor niece was so excited, too—it was supposed to be her very first social event. We bought her a brand new dress for the evening."

Lady Fortinault shot Mary a heartbroken expression. Mary noticed the woman's interest only belatedly, from behind her novel. She forced a desolate expression onto her features; somehow, she managed to make her lip quiver on command. Lady Fortinault now glanced imploringly at her husband—a sturdy fellow in an old military coat.

Lord Fortinault cleared his throat and straightened his back. "Well, this is deplorable," he said. "Really, just a ridiculous situation. I'm sure we can clear it up in just a moment." He turned to fix the majordomo with a haughty, wicked glower.

Lady Navi had chosen her marks well.

"What on earth is the meaning of this?" Lord Fortinault demanded. His posture made it clear that he considered himself the hero of the hour.

The majordomo barely held in a sigh. "My most profuse apologies," he tried. "But the lady has no invitation, and she is not on the list—"

"The lady certainly *should* be on the list," Lord Fortinault snapped. "This is the kumari, Jahnavi Varma. Her family has a long and storied history of service in the Imperial Navy. We had dinner only yesterday. If she is *not* on your list, then I assure you it is some sort of oversight."

The line behind us had grown long and pressing. The majordomo looked past Lord Fortinault's shoulder at the crowd. All at once, his manner deflated.

"Of course, Lord Fortinault," the servant sighed. "Please do go inside, all of you."

Mary brightened, instantly cured of her tears. Navi smiled gratefully at Lord Fortinault, drawing herself up with salvaged dignity.

Lady Navi had never needed an invitation in her life. Privileged indignation, carefully applied, had always served her admirably.

* * *

In Avalon, conspicuous aether consumption was a common method of displaying wealth. This was even more true for the city of Lyonesse, dependent as it was on the grace and skill of its aethermancers.

Chateau Bonaventure was brimming with aether.

Charged crystals in chandeliers flickered with ghostly aether-light —too faint to be of use for anything other than aesthetic purposes. More golden aether-lamps lined the halls to remedy the shortfall of light. Aether was conspicuous in other, more indirect ways; the gold leaf panelling on the vaulted ceilings had bleached from long exposure, and the dark marble floors were broadly veined with white.

I couldn't remember the last time I'd been so surrounded by aether. Even the Imperial Navy had rationed aether more sensibly. Surely, I thought, the attendees had to see how desperately gauche this all was—it was rather like watching someone eat off of an ugly plate made of solid gold.

But no—I heard Lord and Lady Fortinault ahead of me, murmuring with Navi about the good old days. "Do you remember when we all lived like this?" Lady Fortinault sighed. "What a state we've come to. I hope the Coalition is enjoying the fruits of its ridiculous rebellion—less aether for everyone, and a terrible economy on top of that. It's probably even worse in the backwater provinces, like Carrain."

I had to work not to roll my eyes at that. I very much doubted if Lady Fortinault had ever seen Carrain with her own eyes, even before the Sundering War.

"Carrain is actually doing quite well for itself," Mr Finch said, from his place on Navi's arm. "It remains the breadbasket of the continent, you know, and it's leveraged that to negotiate several favourable trade contracts—"

Navi elbowed Finch very delicately in the side, cutting him off. "But of course, you must live rather like a destitute halcyon in Carrain," she said, with false waspishness. "I hear they build their homes into the *ground* there, can you imagine?"

Lady Navi knew how to play to her audience. Lady Fortinault

made a soft sound of disgust. Lord Fortinault shook his head, as though he'd heard a tragic bit of news.

"I've changed my mind," Strahl muttered next to me, from behind his helmet. "They can hang me. I can't believe I have to listen to this all evening."

I glanced quickly around us to see if anyone had heard him. I needn't have bothered; bodyguards and servants were effectively invisible to the upper-crust.

"Lyonesse certainly is in its own little world, isn't it?" I murmured back.

The conversation might have continued, except that we came into the foyer, where several Lyonguard stood at attention. The guards blocked off access to two spiralling staircases leading upwards; more of them patrolled the upper floor, which was open to view from the entranceway. These Lyonguard were dressed somewhat more ceremonially than the ones I'd seen in the plaza... but they were still armed for conflict.

"Interesting," I said under my breath.

"Lots of guards for a little ol' party," Mary whispered to me from behind her book.

"Do they know your *friend* is an important prisoner?" I asked Strahl softly.

I couldn't see Strahl's expression behind the helmet—but I heard the wariness in his voice. "No," he said. "If they knew who she was, there'd be far more than this."

"They could be worried about the silverware," Mary observed. She kept her tone neutral, but I caught a hint of analytical interest in the statement. Every halfway-decent thief knew that good silverware was easy to steal and easy to sell... and Mary's literary addictions were far from cheap.

"I already promised we'd buy you another book after this, Mary," I said warily.

Mary smiled placidly, and turned another page in her novel. "You said we're never coming back to Lyonesse again, either way," she mused. "And just a few of those spoons would buy an *awful* lot of books."

I groaned. "We'll buy you *two* books," I told her. "But you have to leave the silverware alone."

"No silverware," Mary said innocently. "Understood."

She picked up her pace just enough to take Mr Finch by his other arm, and I sighed heavily. Silverware was probably the least expensive thing here, after all.

We followed the river of people through a cavernous hallway between the spiral staircases. From up ahead, we heard the rumbling susurrus of a larger crowd, mixed with the lilting sound of fanciful music.

As we came out into the ballroom, our entire group paused for an extended moment.

"Oh," Navi observed, in a tone that implied she'd discovered something quaint. "That's rather pretty, isn't it?"

Ahead of us, among the sea of powdered wigs and shimmering ball gowns, an armada of tables floated upon the air. Inside the opalescent glass of the furniture, aether sparked and roiled, lighting up the tablecloths from below. Aether-bleached placemats and frosted white wine glasses balanced on the tables, along with—oh dear, the *silverware*.

There was so much silverware. I counted at least twelve pieces per seat—several forks and spoons of varying sizes, two knives, and a claw-like contraption whose purpose probably only Navi knew.

I sneaked a worried glance at Mary... but her eyes, I found, were fixed on something *else*.

The principal attraction of each table was a singular centrepiece: a tall, spiky plant that I had never seen before. Navi let out an impressed sort of *hm* as she saw the centrepieces. Mr Finch let out a gasp of delight.

"Pineapples!" Finch breathed. The man's congenitally pinched face took on an expression of child-like wonder. "Goodness, there are so many of them!"

"Pine... what?" I asked in a low tone.

Strahl grunted next to me, unimpressed. "Pineapples," he said flatly. "They're fruit."

"An *expensive* fruit," Mary added, in a suspiciously upbeat tone. "Ooh, look how many there are!"

"A… fruit?" I frowned at the closest plant. "I've never seen one of those on a pine tree before."

"They don't come from pines," Strahl said.

"So why call them…" I shook my head in confusion. "Never mind. You know, they don't look particularly appetising."

"People don't generally eat them, anyway," Strahl informed me stonily.

I shot his helmet an incredulous look. "What on earth is the point, then?" I asked. "They're not even pretty to look at!"

"Having pineapples shows you're rich," Mary told me patiently. "I saw one in a fancy hotel once."

"Someone probably rented the lot of them for the party," Strahl said. His voice implied the same level of disgust I currently felt.

"I'm… sorry," I said slowly. "You can *rent* fruit?"

Mr Finch must have heard us conversing, for he soon released Navi's arm and dropped back to speak to me. "I always wondered what a pineapple would taste like," he said in an excited whisper. "We had one in the house once. My sister dared me to cut it open. My father caught us just as I'd made the *barest* of incisions. That scent! It's haunted me to this day!" He kept his tone low, as though he were conveying a shameful scandal rather than a story about a piece of fruit.

Mary clapped a lacy glove over her mouth to hide her laughter. But I didn't miss the way her eyes glimmered at the pineapples that surrounded us.

"And how much would a pineapple *sell* for," I asked carefully, "given that the richest people in Lyonesse must rent them?"

"Oh, it depends where you buy one, of course," Mr Finch said dreamily. "They grow in abundance in particular regions of the Rust, but you need to grow them in a hothouse almost anywhere else. Here at the centre of the continent, I'd say a pineapple would cost… about as much as we just spent on repairs, actually."

I missed a step.

"For a piece of fruit," I said. "A piece of fruit that nobody is going to eat."

"Welcome to Lyonesse," Strahl muttered.

I shook my head, trying to dispel my pineapple fury. Mr Finch gave the nearest piece of fruit another look of open longing. Mary, meanwhile, had begun to studiously *ignore* the centrepieces in a way that made me suspect she was already planning a pineapple heist.

I wasn't sure how she'd manage it in that dress, but I'd resigned myself to the fact that she was certainly going to *try*.

The music that we'd heard before came from liveried musicians. As I turned away from the tables, I noticed strings, flutes, and even a harpsichord, all playing with curated formality. Some of the gathered elite had already taken to waltzing at the centre of the ballroom. Above them, a vast artificial sky glittered with aether crystals crafted to resemble stars. I nearly observed that there was a perfectly sufficient night sky *outside*—but I stifled the thought, aware that Mr Finch was already speculating on how the engineers had accomplished the feat. Sometimes, it's just best to let people enjoy things.

Tall windows made up the entire length of the western wall; their metal frames were artistically rendered to represent the four Winds of Fortune, the heralds of the Seelie Tuath Dé. Most prominent, of course, was five-winged Tiirdan, the herald of Death Victorious. The great thunderbird's wings rose above the other three heralds, as though to imply he had overcome them. The Benefactor's herald, Caphea, had been portrayed as a small, shy thing in the corner. Mercy, I thought, was not high on the list of virtues in good old Lyonesse.

Small glass doors led out through the windows, onto a balcony overlooking the gardens. I caught sight of other tables hovering there, lit by a hundred flickering candles.

"So, Mr Strahl," I murmured. "Any thoughts on where we might find your missing comrade?"

Strahl clanked thoughtfully for a few moments as his helmeted gaze swept the room. He soon paused, staring at the centre of the ballroom.

A large, white-streaked brass statue rose above the dancers. It was another proud, intimidating image of Tiirdan. The thunderbird perched atop a seal of polished metal, inlaid into the marble floor. The South Wind's aether-bleached eyes stared over the ballroom, as though surveying the horizon.

"She's under there," Strahl said. He spoke with a peculiar conviction. "There must be a basement... or maybe a secret door."

I furrowed my brow. "How on earth would you know that?" I asked.

Strahl stayed silent for a moment. At first, I thought he might not answer—but finally, he spoke again. "We're connected by an Oath," he said quietly. "A special one."

His tone implied he wouldn't be elaborating further. I accepted the answer for what it was.

"I see," I said dryly. "In which case, we only need to sneak our way through a secret door in the middle of a bustling dance floor." I glanced sideways at Mr Finch. "Is there any chance you and Mary could get a closer look?" I asked.

Mr Finch stroked nervously at his chin. "A secret door at the centre of a ballroom seems unlikely," he said. "And there are all of those *people*—"

I turned to Mary. "Can you and Mr Finch get a closer look?" I asked her, deadpan.

"Well," Mr Finch scoffed. "I say!"

"On it, Cap'n," Mary said, in a stately tone. "Just leave it to me." *The Strange Adventures of Jack Blue* had somehow disappeared from her hand—though I wasn't sure just where she'd hidden it. Mary looped an arm through Mr Finch's with an exaggerated, childlike haughtiness. "Come along, my good man!" she said.

Mary dragged my chief engineer away, in a flurry of bright ruffles and lace.

"Your niece seems to have stolen your escort, Kumari," Lady

Fortinault observed with a hint of bemusement, as Mary dragged Mr Finch out onto the dance floor. "What an adorable thing she is."

"She has certainly inherited her fair share of the family charm," Navi said proudly. I suspected her pride was genuine, though the familial relation was pure fiction. The gunnery ladies were a tight-knit sort, and Navi had long since adopted the rest of the women as a sort of replacement for the family she had lost in the war.

"Would you like to join us at our table, Kumari?" Lord Fortinault asked Navi graciously. His chest was still puffed up from his previous gallantry, and he seemed determined to double down on his newfound chivalry.

"Nothing would delight me more," Navi declared. "I had been thinking that last night's supper was far too short a time to spend in your company. I cannot tell you how much I've missed such sparkling conversation."

Lord Fortinault glanced knowingly towards me and Strahl. I tried not to raise my hackles at the superior look in his eyes.

We reached the table in question—after which time, there was a long, drawn-out pause. Navi flicked her eyes towards me, and I lunged belatedly to pull out a chair for her.

"Thank you very much, William," Navi said. She spoke to me with the same fond, parental tone that so many nobles used with their goblin servants—as though I were a child in training.

I briefly wished that Navi weren't such an accomplished actress. That tone made my skin crawl.

"You're welcome, Your Ladyship," I mumbled obligingly. I reminded myself forcibly that meek, obedient servants were easy to overlook.

Navi patted me on the head and settled into her chair. That should have been the end of anyone's interest in me—but Lady Fortinault kept her eyes upon me for some reason.

"It really must be fate that we ran into one another again, Kumari," she said. "I had such a regret after you left, last night. I've decided that I mustn't allow this second opportunity to pass."

Navi raised her eyebrows at this. "Oh?" she asked curiously. "I don't know what you could mean by that."

Lady Fortinault smiled indulgently. "I understand you've enjoyed travelling the continent," she said. "But surely, if there were anywhere you might take a pause, it would be Lyonesse. Lord Fortinault and I would be only too pleased to have you as our guest for an extended period."

Her gaze lingered on me, and I suddenly knew I was about to become a topic of conversation.

"That little darling niece of yours would be welcome too, of course," Lady Fortinault continued. "Though... I will admit, we do not currently require any further servants. And we *do* try not to employ Oathbroken help."

I carefully pretended not to hear her.

"Oh," Navi said. The offer had clearly taken her aback. "How very... kind of you, Lady Fortinault."

The sole evidence of Navi's scorn was a brief, nearly unnoticeable pause.

"I must admit," Navi observed finally, "you do remind me an awful lot of my youngest son's wife." She smiled warmly, and Lady Fortinault preened at the observation.

This, I knew, was not a compliment. Lady Navi had despised her late son's pretentious wife.

"I will seriously consider your offer," Navi assured the woman. "I *have* enjoyed my time here so far... and of course, my niece could do with further exposure to good society."

Lady Fortinault beamed at this. "I know so very many people who would love to meet you," she said. "Why, I'll have to introduce you around while we're here—"

Murmurs rose in the crowd, and the noblewoman cut herself off abruptly, fixing her eyes just past Navi's shoulder.

I followed Lady Fortinault's gaze to the ballroom's entrance.

A lone figure had entered the room, clad in fine grey and silver apparel. His half cape and high-collared jacket struck me as vaguely

Imperial, though the clothing was far too fashionable to be a military uniform. Lengthy tubes of silver ran from a polished breastplate at his chest to the gauntlets at his hands. Some of the tubes disappeared beneath his cape, implying other foci somewhere upon his person. His hair had aged white before the rest of him; bright blue veins stood out upon his face, like strange marbling.

The old numeral for *one* had been embroidered upon his cape, marking him as Warden Alistair Drayton—the First of the City.

"I wasn't aware that the other wardens were coming tonight!" Lady Fortinault murmured in shock.

I swallowed a small sound of distress.

"I… wasn't aware that they were coming either," Navi said warily. The statement, I knew, was meant for me and not for Lady Fortinault.

"What an interesting party this is going to be!" Lady Fortinault said. She smiled winningly at Navi. "I'm so very glad you're here for it."

Two men of similar dignity soon walked in behind the first.

One, clad in startling scarlet, stood head and shoulders above the other two. If I hadn't been able to see his pale, bearded face, I might have assumed that he was a hobgoblin. Long, platinum hair cascaded down his shoulders in a thick, leonine mane; a web of blue veins covered his hands and neck, standing out against his skin. He wore mechanical plate armour, too heavy to be purely ceremonial. His half cape, stylised with a gold, enumerated III, marked him as Warden Gordian Ferric, Third of the City.

The last man—tall, slender, and curiously unarmoured—was nearly as unnoticeable as his heraldic counterpart on the windows. Though he wore a faded gentleman's waistcoat and cravat, he walked with a casual, distracted sort of grace, in a way that made him nearly blend in with the servants. His silver hair and cerulean half cape set him apart, however, and the vivid blue veins that crawled up his jaw clashed with his deep olive skin. The numeral at his shoulder marked him as Warden Loric Ravenelle, the Fourth of the City.

Warden Albright, Second of the City, strode through the crowd of dancers to meet her latest guests. The thundercloud on her face implied that she was less than happy to see them.

There were only four wardens of Lyonesse—all aethermancers of exceptional, unparalleled skill—and all four of them had decided to join the party.

4

TIIRDAN'S TREASURY - NOT A STICK -
MURDEROUS INTENTIONS - CHOOSING
A FOOL

Warden Jasmine Albright, Second of the City, looked different when she wasn't trying to murder me.

She was a bit younger than I'd originally assumed. Her face was smooth, and she had a vigour to her stride that the other wardens lacked. Her sable hair was threaded with silver, rather than fully bleached, but I suspected it would be snowy white before the year was over. She'd pulled most of the hair back into a fighting braid and pinned it atop her head, though wild wisps escaped confinement here and there. Spidery blue veins rose up the sun-kissed skin of her throat, casting strange tendrils across her cheek. Her eyes were a dead, dishwater grey, drained of all their colour.

The last time I'd seen Warden Albright, she'd bleached her ink-black apparel to a murky grey—but tonight, she was wearing fresh blacks. Her masculine style set her instantly apart from the other ladies present; her trousers were practical, if formal, and the spurs on her heavy boots jingled with each step. Tight, silver coils banded her arms beneath her dark half cape. At her belt, she carried several aethermancer's trinkets, along with a coiled whip. A pair of goggles fashioned like a bird of prey rested just atop her head.

She looked nearly as unhappy to be at the party as I was.

55

"What an honour," Warden Albright drawled, as she paused before the other three wardens. "Can't imagine what brought y'all to my little party." She smiled thinly. "You want some little sandwiches? I think we've got some little sandwiches."

I laughed louder than I should have done.

Unfortunately, the rest of the room had fallen dramatically silent. My single *Ha!* was deafening in the stillness. Several people turned to look at me, aghast.

I glanced quickly to Mr Strahl, schooling my face into a stricken expression. Disapproving looks diverted his way. He endured them silently, with apparent indifference.

"No sandwiches then," Warden Albright observed. "You let me know if you change your minds."

The reality of the situation slowly settled in, as the tension between the wardens grew.

"There's no way we can pull this off with all four of them here," I whispered to Strahl. "We should use this as a scouting opportunity. We can come back when our… *august* company has departed."

"Waiting is too dangerous," Strahl murmured calmly. "The longer this goes on, the more likely it is they'll realise who they've captured. If I see a chance, I'm taking it."

I suppressed my frustrated response. It was clear that Strahl would not be moved.

Instead, I considered our options.

A whole estate's worth of guards and all four wardens of Lyonesse was… extreme odds. Strahl might be willing to gamble on that, but the rest of us didn't have to join him. We could make our excuses, leave the party, and avoid the coming fireworks entirely.

We'd be out our ace navigator. But really, what navigator could possibly be worth all of this?

I *wanted* to help. That was the problem. The moment Strahl had risked his neck for Evie against an elite aethermancer, I'd decided he was crew. But by the Lady of Fools, there were *limits*.

I caught sight of Mary and Mr Finch returning through the crowd. I sighed. "We'll see what our professionals have to say," I muttered.

The four wardens dropped their voices, just as Mary wove her way back to the table. Mr Finch limped wearily after her, and I suspected then that Mary had insisted on dancing. Strahl and I stepped aside to speak with them both, as Navi carefully held the noble couple's attention.

"Did you find anything?" I whispered.

"We were able to get a closer look at the statue," Mr Finch murmured. "Given the awkward dimensions, I believe a hidden staircase to be incredibly unlikely."

"That's a relief," I sighed. "We're looking for a basement, then. I might be able to ask the other servants about it—"

"However," Mr Finch continued apologetically.

"However?" I asked.

"However!" Mary declared officiously. She snapped open a fan to hide her face as she spoke. I couldn't help but notice that the fan didn't match her dress. "When I dropped a bit of snuff—"

"What are you doing with snuff?" I demanded.

"It wasn't mine," Mary assured me, with a pat on my hand. "Anyway, when I dropped the snuff, a little draft sucked it away between the inlay and the marble."

"It's fine craftsmanship," Mr Finch mused. "I would never have noticed, otherwise."

"So what does this mean?" I hissed at them.

"I believe there's a lift beneath the statue," Mr Finch said. "A *small* lift. I very much doubt if you could fit a person in it."

"A lift?" I muttered. "Awfully strange place to put a lift, isn't it?"

"—know darn well why you're actually here," Warden Albright was saying. Her voice became audible again as she led the other wardens through the crowd, just past our table. "You think I don't know you fellas have spies in this house? Anyway, I'd have been a lot more polite if you'd just *asked* to see it. But no, I guess we get to play these fool games instead."

Warden Albright walked towards the statue at the centre of the ballroom.

"Since you been so impolite about it," she continued, "I'm goin' to let you take a peek—*once.*" She smiled bitterly. "After that, you'll have to duel me. And let me tell you, boys, I'm not like to pull my punches after tonight."

Warden Albright shooed away the guests on the dance floor. It didn't take much doing—four aethermancers in one spot was generally enough to scare off most reasonable people. She stepped in front of the statue and lifted her armour-clad arm. The contraption there vented a gout of prismatic aether; lightning danced across its gleaming metal, running down to pool in the warden's palm. Warden Albright's eyes sparked brightly. She exhaled once, and a plume of cool blue light passed her lips—then, the bolt of aether twisted from her hand, arcing into Tiirdan's statue.

Aether flashed and cracked. The whine of charged aether made my bones rattle and my teeth ache, even from a distance. A few of the guests had hovered just close enough to eavesdrop on the wardens; now, they scattered back like ants. I suspected that some of the nosier nobles would be nursing headaches soon. Maybe, I thought, that had been Warden Albright's intention. She'd shown a tad bit more control of her aether when I'd tangled with her, after all.

The other wardens didn't flinch back, however. They stood next to Warden Albright, as rooted as stone. Warden Drayton and Warden Ferric withstood the discomfort with stony expressions. Warden Ravenelle flicked a finger across his worn waistcoat, as though brushing away a bit of lint; a small circle of calm opened around him, as little arcs of lightning diverted themselves from his person.

A great mechanical noise rumbled beneath our feet. Tiirdan's statue rose slowly from the floor, stretching its five wings in triumph. Lightning sparked against its feathers—and for a second, its eyes glowed so fiercely that I imagined it was real.

A small, self-contained glass chamber rose from the floor beneath the statue. Inside it were a handful of mismatched curios and pieces of jewellery—relics of the Imperium, I realised, preserved for posterity.

It wasn't a lift, after all—it was a display case.

At the centre of the display, there hovered a single object of simple, breathtaking beauty. It was a knotted staff of polished wood, as thick as my arm and a full head taller than I was. A riot of budding flowers like those that lined the streets of Lyonesse bloomed at the tip of the wood, rustling silently in the aetheric field that held the staff aloft. The staff made me think of a driftwood ballerina, though there was no visible anatomy to suggest such a thing.

It was one of the most exquisite things I'd ever seen. I should have felt awed by it—startled by its elegance.

I didn't expect to feel... angry.

It was a strange, pervasive feeling—it wafted over the ballroom like a subtle perfume. The more I stared at the staff, the more I felt it in my bones, impossible to ignore.

I wasn't the only one feeling it, either.

"One might expect that you would be more forthcoming with something of such consequence to the city, Jasmine," said Warden Drayton. His tone was light and honeyed, but his rigid posture implied irritation.

"Forgot my title already, have you?" Warden Albright snapped. "That didn't take long, now did it?" She vented aether from her foci, and the stormy sensation in the room slowly abated. Little arcs of aetheric blue lightning still danced over her arm, but they now seemed tighter and more controlled. "I'd been plannin' on studyin' the thing until I knew what to tell you. And there was the small matter of me settin' up a funeral." Her voice cracked with fury. "Take a look, Warden Drayton. There's a faerie artefact if I ever saw one. An' now, you ain't never gonna touch it unless you want to fight me for it."

Her gauntlet snarled with a harsh pop of lightning, punctuating the words.

Tensions rose around us. I stared at the four wardens, deeply uneasy. Something here wasn't quite right. I felt boxed in—suffocated. I felt like everyone was staring at me, *judging* me. It made me want to hurt someone... or *everyone*.

"Please tell me your friend is not a stick," I mumbled at Strahl.

"That is not a stick," Strahl said grimly.

Conversations rose in volume around us, suddenly tinged with indignation. Tempers flared. I started feeling nauseous, keenly aware of the walls closing in on me, in spite of the room's generous size. The painted faces around me inspired a deep and terrible loathing.

Loathing? Where had that come from?

Strahl walked through the crowd towards the display case. Irrational anger surged through me again, and I hurried after him. "Where are you going?" I hissed. My head pounded with dizziness. One of the noble ladies bumped into me; her outraged curses followed me, heavy with scorn. Hateful eyes turned to watch me as I went, tempered only by the heavily armoured presence just in front of me.

Strahl stopped at the edge of the circle that had formed around the glass display case. I heard murmurs of surprise behind us, just as I caught up with him. One of the ladies in attendance had fainted.

Some instinct made me glance back towards Mary. My heart leaped into my throat as I saw her waver on her feet—but Mr Finch caught her quickly and guided her to a nearby chair. A sharp sense of alarm cut through the alien fury in my mind, snapping me out of the strange reverie that now gripped the entire room.

I snatched at Mr Strahl's wrist, closing my fingers around the gauntlet there. I tried to haul him back, but I was obviously unequal to the task; he proved as immovable as a mountain. Still, Strahl turned his head to regard me.

"Tell me what is going on," I hissed at him. "Now. Otherwise, I am taking my crew and we are leaving."

Strahl inclined his helmet reluctantly. "Let me calm her down first," he murmured.

He reached into a pouch with his hand and produced a dried flower. It looked painfully delicate against his armoured palm.

"Syrene," Strahl whispered.

The name was barely loud enough for me to hear it—but as he spoke it, something changed in the air. The tension bled away abruptly, replaced by a soaring hope. The crowd around the display case calmed for a moment.

The staff had stopped spinning.

"That is definitely not a stick," I whispered. Worry dawned upon me, and I knew this time that it was entirely my own.

"You're right," Strahl said softly. "Syrene is a faerie." His eyes stared out from the helmet, fixed upon the display case. "Captain Blair—meet Syrene."

The hovering staff turned slightly to face me. From a certain angle, I realised, the dancing flowers at the top looked more like hair.

I was in the presence of a faerie—a genuine servant of the holy Tuath Dé.

And I'd called her a stick.

I waved hesitantly at the confined faerie.

"Um," I said, beneath my breath. "Hello."

The faerie, of course, did not respond.

I dragged Strahl back from the edge of the dance floor. This time, he allowed me to do it.

"You might have mentioned before now that your friend was a faerie," I hissed at him, once we'd escaped the press of people and reached the far wall.

"Would you have believed me?" Strahl asked stonily.

I wanted to say yes… but we both knew that would be more than a bit silly. I stayed silent instead, thinking through the implications.

There's not another navigator like Syrene in all of Avalon, Strahl had told me. It was no wonder he'd been so confident about that. Faeries were quite literally not of our world; in fact, the four most powerful Seelie faeries were said to have *created* our world from the raw aether of Arcadia. Most people never caught so much as a glimpse of a faerie during their lifetime, unless they were venturing into truly wild territories. Neither did most people *want* to meet a faerie. Even those faeries who meant humans well were often too alien to *do* them well—and not all faeries served the four holy Tuath Dé.

"What happens if the wardens figure out what they've caught?" I asked quietly.

Strahl took a deep breath. "Nothing good," he said. "Syrene has a history with the Imperium. Warden Clovis would have used her as a symbol to rally support. He wanted to turn Lyonesse into the capital of a new Imperium—to bring back the good old days."

My blood ran cold at the suggestion.

"You killed him before he could tell anyone," I whispered. "Warden Clovis *did* know who Syrene was, didn't he?"

"He was the oldest warden of Lyonesse," Strahl said grimly. "And apparently still nostalgic for the Imperium. I have to wonder how many of the other wardens share that nostalgia."

This was... far more than I had bargained for. I could barely conceive of the consequences we were dealing with.

"I'm not interested in finding out the answer to that question," Strahl said softly.

He didn't ask me whether I wanted to see a new Imperium. He already knew that I didn't. I'd insisted on telling him myself, entirely unprompted.

"I need to tell the others," I said.

"The more people you tell," Strahl said, "the more likely it is that someone will find out." He tugged his arm from my grip. "Help me get her back, Captain. We'll join your crew and be forgotten—as we should be."

I looked back over the room with a sinking feeling. Even now, several Lyonguard watched the gathering from the exits. Four wardens of Lyonesse still stood between me and the very angry stick —er, faerie—at the centre of the dance floor.

The odds were near-impossible.

"Rot and ruin," I groaned. "I should have left you to hang."

I didn't really mean the words. I just needed to complain. But Strahl shrugged in agreement. "You probably should have," he admitted.

"But that wouldn't change what's going on," I muttered morosely. "Syrene would still be here. There'd just be no one to spring her before the wardens figured things out." I glanced up accusingly at the sky of artificial stars. "You're a cruel mistress," I told the Lady of Fools. "You'd better be ready to help me with this."

"I'm a what?" Strahl asked me.

"Not you," I snapped. "Never mind. I don't know how we're going to pull this off yet. Give me time to think." I turned to head back toward my crew, to check on poor Mary.

Mr Finch had found a nearby chair for Mary and settled her into it, as gallant would-be gentlemen crowded around loudly expressing their concern for her. Mr Finch had picked up Mary's mysteriously-acquired fan; he now used it alternately to fan at her and to swat irritatedly at the crowd of buzzing nobles. Lady Navi spoke a few words to the gathered men, putting on her best *winsome old woman* expression; within moments, she had diverted them to various tasks. At least two separate men went in search of punch, while another went on the hunt for a physicker. As I came closer, however, I saw that my youngest gunnery lady was already awake.

"Ooh, good you did that, Navi," Mary sighed, as she tugged at the top of her dress. "I think I was about to kill one of them."

I blinked at this. Mary was far from averse to violence when the situation called for it, but there was something strange about her tone.

"Kill one of them?" I echoed slowly. I stopped perhaps a step or two further away than I'd planned.

Mary tried to sit up as she saw me, but Mr Finch held her shoulder against the chair with a stern look.

"I can't explain it, Cap'n," Mary said in a low voice. "I was just standing there. Then suddenly, I got so... angry. I felt like the room was too small and everyone was staring at me. I really wanted to hurt someone." She paused thoughtfully. "I was just so angry I forgot to breathe, I think."

I let out a slow breath. "You weren't the only one," I muttered. I glanced at Navi and Mr Finch. "Did either of you feel it?"

Navi smiled grimly. "I did," she said. "It passed so quickly that I thought it must be normal party nerves."

I raised my eyebrows at her. "Do you mean to say you *normally* feel homicidal at parties?" I asked.

Navi scoffed. "Need I remind you, Captain, that I have been conducting small talk with that awful couple nearly since we got here?" she said.

I turned my laugh into a soft cough. "Point taken," I said.

"I was angry for a moment as well," Mr Finch admitted. "But I didn't question it until now, for some reason. What *was* that? And why would Mary be so much more affected than the rest of us?"

I knitted my brow. "I think… because she's younger?" I guessed. Mary shot me an annoyed look, and I held up my hands. "You're at an, er, stage in life where you're more emotional, dear. Don't murder me, or you'll prove my point."

Navi glanced around the room surreptitiously. "Mary is the youngest person here by far," she observed. "But some of the other young ladies look faint. I believe one of the younger men in the corner over there might have thrown fists."

"The older people here haven't even realised they were affected," I said slowly. "That's… a bit frightening, actually."

The thought sank in slowly as I considered my crew in front of me.

"So." I cleared my throat carefully. "The good news is that I know where Mr Strahl's friend is being kept."

Mary raised her eyebrows at that—forgetting, for the moment, her irritation with me. "That's helpful!" she said. "Is she locked up somewhere? I *did* make sure to bring my lockpicks."

"Oh, splendid," Mr Finch sighed. "Do you think we could finish this and escape before the end of the party?"

Navi was far too canny to celebrate prematurely. She crossed her arms and waited, raising both her eyebrows at me.

I sighed. "The bad news is that Mr Strahl's friend is the stick. Er, I mean—she's a faerie." I shot another apologetic look towards the display case, in case Syrene had somehow heard me. "So, our prisoner is in that display case, surrounded by the city's four most powerful, battle-hardened aethermancers."

Silence settled in for a moment.

One of the noble gentlemen returned with a delicate flute of punch. Navi took the drink and downed it in one smooth swallow.

"I don't taste any alcohol," she murmured. "Blast it. Would you be a dear and find this old woman something stronger? It's medicinal, you know. For my nerves."

I let the situation stew in my mind as Navi chased the nobleman away once more.

"A real faerie?" Mary murmured. A hint of wonder slipped into her voice. She arched up from her chair to look at the display case, just past my shoulder.

Mr Finch had blanched. He now began to fan at himself, unthinking. My chief engineer might have been an academic, but he'd thrown in his lot with the Coalition during the war. A small number of faeries had directly supported the Tuath-blessed Imperium. The Coalition had no doubt had plenty of reason to swap faerie stories around the fire... and none of them, I'd hazard, had been pleasant.

Worse, I realised—Syrene probably *was* one of the faeries that had terrorised the Coalition, according to Strahl's comments.

None of it could be helped. Whatever Syrene had done before, she couldn't stay here with the wardens. If they wanted to raise a new Imperium, they would have to do it without her.

Navi returned, shaking her head. "A faerie," she murmured. "I can't decide whether we're cursed or blessed, Captain. Either way, it's never a dull moment with you." She glanced sideways at Strahl. "I take it we are effecting a rescue despite the difficulties, since we've yet to flee the premises?"

"We are," I said gloomily. "It's important. And... it's probably best if I don't tell you why."

I had asked dangerous things from my crew before—there was no avoiding that sort of thing on a ship like ours. But I generally preferred to discuss our choices out in the open, with complete honesty. I greatly disliked asking them to walk into danger without an explanation. Nor was I entirely certain that they *would* do so.

Navi considered me for a long moment. Finally, however, she inclined her head. "I believe you, Captain," she said softly. "Very well. Our rescue mission continues."

I looked around at the other faces in our group. I had expected *someone* to push back against the idea that we ought to pursue this impossible heist on my word alone. Rather than protests, however, I received only expectant silence.

That sort of trust was awe-inspiring… and, if I'm truly honest, just a little bit frightening.

I sucked in a breath. "Well—unfortunately, we have to do this tonight. Warden Albright's made it clear that she's going to lock down that display case as soon as the party is over." I rubbed at my face. I'd firmly decided that we had to spring the faerie from lock-up—but the odds were still impossible.

I started counting off our resources in my head. They looked sparse, no matter how I considered things—and the dull feeling of claustrophobia I still felt wasn't making it any easier to *think*.

"Syrene is doing this," I said. I addressed the observation behind me, at Strahl. "She's projecting her own emotions on everyone here."

Strahl inclined his head minutely.

"We need to get her to stop," I muttered. "This is hard enough as it is without trying to plan through a headache—" I paused abruptly as something occurred to me.

Several lingering questions had just answered themselves, all at once.

"That's how you defeated Warden Clovis," I hissed. I barely dared to whisper the words. "Syrene distracted him for you."

"An aethermancer who can't focus isn't much of an aethermancer," Strahl said softly. It was as good as a confirmation.

I flipped things around in my mind. Syrene wasn't an obstacle. She was a *resource*.

"So Syrene *can* focus it on one person," I said. "She distracted Clovis, but she didn't distract you." I thought furiously. "How precise is she? Can she project other emotions?"

Strahl shifted thoughtfully on his feet. "Her emotions tend to leak out regardless," he said. "But she can control it when she wants. And… I think she can choose the emotion, yes. She's put the fear of the Tuath Dé into men before, and she certainly wasn't feeling afraid when she did it."

Mr Finch shuddered at this, and I briefly wondered which Coalition horror story he was thinking about.

"This is..." I closed my eyes, thinking. "This might be barely feasible."

I recounted our resources, adding Syrene into the mix. New avenues appeared.

I opened my eyes again. "Lady Navi," I said, "the wardens of Lyonesse don't seem to like one another very much, from what I can tell."

Navi smirked dryly. "Men with power rarely enjoy one another's company," she said. "Though they especially despise *women* with power."

Navi had correctly identified our opening. I couldn't help sending a mental apology to Warden Albright, though she *had* tried to kill me. I had been the scapegoat for so many people's anger and insecurity in my life that it was difficult not to empathise with her position.

Still. We had a faerie to rescue—and the stakes were far higher than one woman's title.

"Tell me more about that," I said. "There's three of them and one of her. If the others really didn't want a female warden, then why was she elevated?"

Navi inclined her head in acknowledgement. "Warden Clovis died abruptly," she said. "Jasmine Albright was his best student, though gossip says he regularly overlooked her talents. His house never would have selected her to succeed him... but Warden Drayton strongly suggested she should have the position. Since he is First of the City, his word obviously carries weight."

"Drayton?" Strahl asked. "That's ridiculous. He's just as stuck in the past as Clovis was."

Navi shot him a pitying look. "Mr Strahl," she said, "please cease speculating on political matters. It does not suit you." She looked back at me. "The houses of Lyonesse duel one another regularly, in order to keep their skills sharp. It's a common spectacle for the nobles here. But the wardens only duel one another personally in order to rise within the city's hierarchy. Warden Drayton has always considered the Ebon Warden's house to be the greatest threat to his position. Warden Clovis had no interest in being First of the City... but several of his underlings would salivate at the thought of the position."

I knitted my brow. "So... Warden Drayton chose Albright *because* he thinks she's weak?" I said. "He wanted to disadvantage her house?"

"Quite," Navi said. "Warden Ferric also holds a low opinion of Albright's skills. Everyone fully expects him to challenge for Second of the City any day now." Her smile turned cat-like. "Dinner conversation suggests that neither man has assessed the situation correctly. Warden Albright defeated her mentor on several occasions. Her house would never have agreed to elevate her if they believed she would damage them."

Confidence grew within me with every word. *We can work with this,* I thought.

"What about the Fourth of the City?" I asked. "Where does he stand in all of this?"

Navi frowned at that. "No one knows," she said. "Warden Ravenelle gave no opinion on the matter of Albright's elevation. The Cerulean Warden has traditionally acted as a peacekeeper between the other wardens—he has always been Fourth of the City. He and his house specialise in defensive aethermancy, which does not lend itself very well to duelling. One expects as much from the Benefactor's house, I suppose."

I remembered the casual way that Warden Ravenelle had defused the aether around him. I was no aethermancer myself, but I knew what confidence looked like. I turned to search the room for him. It didn't take me very long at all.

The man in the faded blue waistcoat still stood at the centre of the room, right next to the display case. A strange bubble of calm surrounded him, so palpable that I could *see* it. The people directly next to him were far more relaxed than they should have been while standing next to that murderous faerie.

"He's our problem," I said. "Warden Ravenelle. You said he's a peacekeeper—I think that's literal. Look at how little Syrene has affected him. He's grounding out her power somehow. I don't think he even realises he's doing it." I let out a breath. "The other three are a powder-keg. With Syrene's help, we could easily set a spark and send this situation spiralling out of control. But as long as Warden Ravenelle is here, he'll interfere."

"Soft power," Navi sighed. "What a bother. Insecure men are far easier to handle."

Mary straightened in her chair, brushing off the front of her dress. She had an enigmatic smile on her face. "Three books," she said.

I blinked at her. "What?" I asked.

"Three books," Mary repeated firmly, "and I'll handle the Cerulean Warden." Her eyes glittered at me. "He looks nice, Captain. Don't you think he looks *nice?*"

I looked sceptically at the man next to the display case. Warden Ravenelle might have been a bit faded-looking, but he certainly didn't look *nice*, with all of those militant aethermancer's accoutrements on his person. He did put off a pleasant demeanour, but I greatly suspected he was capable of just as much violence as the other three wardens, when pressed.

"He looks very nice," Mary repeated innocently. "I've got all sorts of questions I want to ask him."

I suppressed a smile. "I see," I said. "All right. Three books—but that's my final offer. Just be careful, will you? Lenore will have my head if you come back injured."

Mary rolled her eyes, in a moment of pure adolescence. "I'll be *fine*, Captain," she said.

I turned my attention back to the others. "I'll need you to get that display case open, Mr Finch," I said. "It hasn't got a traditional lock on it—it opens with some sort of aethermancy, I'm sure. We're fresh out of aethermancers, so our engineer will have to do."

Mr Finch groaned. "It's right out in the open, Captain," he said. "You can't really ask me to—"

"I *am* asking you," I said. "No one else here can get that case open, Mr Finch. None of us would even know where to begin."

Mr Finch looked pleadingly around at the others—but he received only expectant looks in return.

"You promised me a drink," he told Navi forlornly. "I require a drink."

Navi smiled benevolently at him. "How do we get the case open, dear?" she asked.

Mr Finch shook his head. "The case uses passive aether to make the objects float," he said. "That means it has a small core of aether crystal somewhere inside of it. Warden Albright used her aethermancy to stimulate the core and raise the display case. I expect one could open it using the same method—but none of us can control aether. The best I could do is flood the whole case with aether and hope for the best." He paused. "We don't *have* any aether with us, Captain."

I shot him a dry look. "Look around you, Mr Finch," I said. "There's enough aether in this room to buy another *Iron Rose*. I'm sure you can repurpose some of it."

Mr Finch's expression turned sour, and I knew he had been hoping I wouldn't notice the obvious. "Yes, fine," he said. "I suppose I can try."

"You're a treasure, Mr Finch," Navi told him soothingly.

"That just leaves our distraction," I said. "Warden Ferric is our softest target. He's hungry to take Warden Albright's position. His house follows the Lady of Fools—so let's encourage him to act the fool."

"I believe we should be capable of that, between us," Navi observed to me. "As long as our… young lady… in the display case is willing to cooperate."

"We need her help if this is going to work," I said. I eyed Strahl consideringly. "Do you think Syrene can hear us?" I asked him.

"No," Strahl said. "She recognised me because of our bond, and because I brought one of her flowers with me. But she can't hear through glass any better than we can."

I breathed a mental sigh of relief. Syrene *hadn't* heard me calling her a stick, after all.

"Er, Mr Strahl," Navi asked delicately, "can faeries *read?* I fear it's a question I have never needed to ask before."

"Faeries understand all mortal languages," Strahl said. "Spoken, written, and otherwise."

I widened my eyes.

"*All* mortal languages?" I asked him.

Strahl nodded slowly. "We would have to get painfully close for her to read anything, though," he said. "I don't think that's an option—"

I walked away from him, towards the display case at the centre of the room. I didn't dare force my way through the nobles surrounding it, but I paused well within sight of the glass. I lifted my hand in a standard sign language greeting, just as I would have done for my first mate.

Something shivered on the air. It was hard to define the feeling... but I had the distinct impression I had caught Syrene's attention.

Hello, fair lady, I signed to the faerie. *This party is boring. It will soon be time to depart.*

A slow bubble of curiosity unfurled within me. The feeling wasn't mine.

We might require your assistance, I added.

Curiosity turned to bemusement... and then, to cold, sinister satisfaction.

Our newest crew member was ready to help.

5

THE TROUBLE WITH AETHERMANCERS - MAKING A SPLASH - A CLOSE CALL - A SCANDAL IN SCARLET

Aethermancers are people of incredible mental will. An engineer might tinker with devices meant to channel aether—generally while keeping a careful distance from the aether itself—but while aethermancers do use mechanical foci, it's their direct control of aether which makes them truly terrifying. Mastering the gift of the Tuath Dé requires a strong personality by definition.

Because of this, I knew that the Cerulean Warden, Loric Ravenelle, was far more worrisome than his external appearance might suggest. Manipulating his actions would be no easy feat, even with Syrene's direct aid.

Alas for Warden Ravenelle—I knew that he was both a peacekeeper and a gentleman.

I followed behind Mary as she approached the Cerulean Warden, keeping my gaze low.

"This is just like the time Jack Blue stole a silver sword," Mary mumbled back at me. "He always wins by being clever, you know. He doesn't even have to use his aethermancy most of the time."

I shushed her quickly, glancing around to make sure no one had heard her. We were close enough to Warden Ravenelle that I worried he might have picked up a hint of her words—but he was engaged in conversation with two militant-looking gentlemen in sharply-cut attire. Both men were old enough to have served in the Sundering War, but neither had any shattered Oaths clinging to them, which made such service unlikely. I decided the two men had probably joined Lyonesse's military after the war was over.

Warden Ravenelle was only partially engaged by his conversation, however. His aether-grey eyes kept darting to the display case, lingering upon the curious prize within. There was a slow, thoughtful look on his face that I did not much like.

As Mary and I came within speaking distance, a subtle ringing rose in my ears—the soft whine of the Cerulean Warden's small foci. A shimmer of blue aether rippled in the air around him, barely noticeable. Warden Albright's foci had set my teeth on edge in a way that I'd assumed was normal for aethermancy... but as I entered Warden Ravenelle's aura, I felt every muscle in my body simultaneously relax. Even the weight of Syrene's fury lessened, pushed back by the calm that the Cerulean Warden exuded.

"...understandable, gentlemen," Warden Ravenelle was saying. "I'm sure the Ivory Warden will have an interest in these concerns. I'll bring the matter to him when we next convene."

Now that I was closer, I was struck by how frustratingly ageless the man was. Nothing about Warden Ravenelle's appearance marked him as an old man... but there was *something* about his manner that convinced me he had lived a bit too long. Much like Mr Strahl, there was a distance in his eyes. The polite smile on his lips did much to disguise it, but I had grown up around tired, broken people; I knew it on sight. There was something else beneath that calm aura that shocked me into a halt, however.

Warden Ravenelle was Oathbroken.

The tattered threads of his Oath brushed against my soul like a spider's web; the closer I got to him, the more the feeling made me shudder in instinctive disgust. It was a stronger feeling than the one I probably carried with me. My Oath had been made young and broken long before I'd fully matured... but Loric Ravenelle had broken his

Oath with *intention*. I felt the sharp edges of his dishonour, even beneath the veil of aether he kept around him.

Warden Ravenelle broke off his polite conversation abruptly. He turned, then, to look straight at me.

Our eyes met with a strange, grim sort of understanding. I was close enough to feel his broken Oath... which meant that he was close enough to feel *mine*.

I was expecting to see shame in the warden's eyes. I often felt shame myself, though I knew intellectually that I'd broken my Oath for good reason. But if there was any shame in Ravenelle's manner, it was buried so deep that it might as well not have existed. The broken Oath had done nothing to diminish the Cerulean Warden's iron will... and the obvious power he carried had done much to smooth over people's normal distaste for Oathbreakers.

I had met plenty of other Oathbroken people—mostly Coalition veterans and people from the wrong side of the law. But I felt a surprising, uncomfortable sense of intimacy meeting another Oathbroken person in such a high-class setting. I knew that Warden Ravenelle alone had marked my presence with empathy, rather than with disgust. And, truth be told, I now gave him far more thought than I had meant to do. My mind wandered away from the exigencies of the moment and settled instead upon the man in front of me. What Oath had he broken? Did he ever regret the decision? What was he thinking as he looked back at me, a broken reflection of his own tarnished soul?

I couldn't help my suspicions—though they were perhaps more generous than I should have allowed. The original wardens of Lyonesse had deserted before the war's end, effectively breaking their Oaths to the empire. Originally, I thought they'd simply seen the writing on the wall and decided that a broken Oath was better than death... but perhaps just one of them had turned his back on the war for a different reason.

"I'm so sorry to interrupt," Mary gushed, startling me from my train of thought. "I've just never met an aethermancer before, and I've heard *so* much about the wardens of Lyonesse, and—and it's just such a pleasure to meet a real warden in person!"

Mary's bookish, reserved demeanour had briefly disappeared; she spoke with her best over-the-top upper-class accent, in a perfect blend of embarrassment and barely-contained enthusiasm. Mary blushed nervously, hiding her face behind a dangerously overfull cup of punch as she looked up at the warden with childish awe.

The deluge of words stunned the three men before us. One of the military fellows turned away from Mary with a hint of open contempt on his face, making his excuses to leave the conversation; his manner suggested that he rarely dealt with children. The other man shot Warden Ravenelle a questioning look, taking his cue from the aethermancer.

Ravenelle jerked his gaze away from me, distracted by Mary's interruption. He smiled patiently at her.

"The pleasure is all mine," the Cerulean Warden said, with utmost sincerity. "May I have your name, miss?"

Mary twittered with such obvious delight that I wondered if some of it wasn't genuine. "I'm Mariah Gwendolyn Varma," she said in a rush. "Oh, but everyone just calls me Mary. I came with my auntie Jahnavi. I can't believe it's only my very first ball and there's *four* famous aethermancers here! You're all so handsome, too—or, oh, do you think Warden Albright would be insulted if I called her handsome? I hope that's not insulting. She *is* all smart-looking in her uniform, isn't she? You just look like such a gentleman, sir—a real hero, just like one of those Silver Legionnaires."

I would have had to be an idiot to miss the flash of discomfort that crossed Warden Ravenelle's face at the mention of Silver Legionnaires. The Avalon Imperium's elite aethermancers had lost some of their heroic sheen since the empire's fall, much like the wargear had done. I noted that discomfort with keen interest, though —if Ravenelle held no love for Silver Legionnaires, then he probably held even less love for faeries like Syrene, who had allied themselves with the Imperium.

Not all of the wardens here are longing for the old days, then, I thought. *I was right about him.*

"I suspect Warden Albright would be just as charmed as I am," Ravenelle told Mary, smoothing over his brief discomposure. "I could introduce you to her, if you like—"

"Does it hurt you to use aether?" Mary asked, rushing straight past the poor warden's attempts to pawn her off. "I heard aethermancers breathe it in, or sometimes they inject it with *needles!*" Her voice rose with panicked horror. "That just sounds awful, I can't imagine. I'm afraid of needles, you know. I'd faint right away if someone tried to inject me with aether! Ooh, even the thought has me a little bit green. You don't use needles, do you, Warden Ravenelle?"

Warden Ravenelle might have had an iron will... but I was now certain that he had never tangled before with a child Mary's age. He blinked quickly, trying to keep up with the flurry of questions and statements as they came and went.

Mary now mimicked Navi's earlier behaviour with the majordomo with a subtle, vicious glee. I knew she was consciously practicing the older woman's advice.

Polite quarry is easy to corner, Navi often said. *You can keep a polite person tied up in knots for days, as long as you show no mercy and take no pauses.*

"I... I assure you, er, it's quite painless, Miss Mary—" Warden Ravenelle attempted.

"Oh no," Mary moaned, cutting him off. "You really *do* use needles? That's just terrible, I can't even think of it—"

The second gentleman in Warden Ravenelle's company now beat a hasty retreat, leaving the aethermancer to face Mary alone.

Warden Ravenelle turned a pleading look on *me* now, and I blinked. I could tell from his expression that he expected I might have some special sway over Mary—maybe even enough to rescue him and divert her attention.

I smiled at him, feigning helplessness.

"I don't think I would use the word *needles,*" Warden Ravenelle reassured Mary desperately. A small, silver contraption on his hand whirred to life, and a narrow tube glowed blue beneath his sleeve. His eyes flickered with light; a wisp of opalescent aether wafted from his lips, like smoke from a pipe. The aura of calm around us intensified, and I suspected he had resorted to aethermancy in an attempt to soothe the small girl in front of him. "You could call them injectors, perhaps—"

Mary gave a girlish squeal of delight. She pointed at the plume of prismatic aether, bouncing on her heels in a way that made the punch in her glass slosh dangerously. "What was that?" she gasped.

Warden Ravenelle held up his hands, as though dealing with a wild animal that might attack him at any moment. "What was what?" he asked warily.

"The smoke!" Mary pressed. "Was that real aethermancy?"

Warden Ravenelle took in a deep, steadying breath; as he exhaled, another trickle of aether left his lips. "Er, yes. It was aether—"

"—mancy!" Mary finished for him, with wide eyes. "It's a bit tingly, isn't it? Is that what aether feels like? I was feeling faint earlier, but I don't think it was because of any aether. Mr Finch was nice enough to catch me, but he's Auntie Navi's escort, you know, and I would have preferred another handsome man to catch me. You're a real hero and a gentleman, I'm *sure* you would have done it if you'd been nearby."

Warden Ravenelle was so turned around by the conversation now that he made his last foolish mistake. "I'm sure I would," he said wearily.

Mary gasped with delight. "You *would?*" she said.

Then—before anyone could protest—she let herself fall towards the floor like a chopped tree.

Warden Ravenelle widened his eyes in terror. My own heart leapt into my chest; Mary had told me she'd *distract* the warden, but she hadn't fully explained how.

The warden had excellent reflexes, thank the Lady—he lunged forward to catch Mary beneath the arms, just as she was halfway to the floor.

The punch in Mary's hand spattered across them both. It stained the flower petals on Mary's hand-sewn dress; it sank with ease into the washed-out blue of Warden Ravenelle's attire. I winced on behalf of my old curtains.

"Mariah Gwendolyn Varma, what *are* you doing?"

Navi's weathered voice cracked across the floor, hot with indignation.

Mary looked up from her awkward place in the warden's arms, suddenly sheepish. She pushed back up to her feet, turning stricken eyes upon Warden Ravenelle, who now glanced down at his clothing with a wince.

"Oh no," Mary moaned. "It's all my fault, I'm so sorry! I really wasn't thinking sir—"

Hard metal fingers curled around Mary's arm, hauling her up onto her tiptoes. Powerful aether hummed around us, strong enough to cut through the Cerulean Warden's aura of calm.

"This isn't a nursery, little girl. Who let you through that door?"

The voice that spoke was old and distinguished, and full of self-importance. It was the tone of a man who knew that everyone present was obliged to give him deference.

Warden Alistair Drayton, First of the City, stared down at Mary with violent disgust.

Mary quailed, shrinking back from the warden's touch—but his iron grip pinched at her arm, holding her fast. Real fear flickered behind her eyes. That fear stoked a quiet anger inside of me.

You can always tell the quality of a man by the way he treats less powerful people. Warden Drayton looked down at Mary with such casual, contemptuous hatred that I knew he considered her more of a *thing* than a person. He had probably arranged his own life such that he rarely needed to keep company with children; Mary's presence was, in his mind, a kind of personal insult.

The most powerful man in the city had Mary in his grip. Based on her soft whimper, I knew he was going to leave bruises.

"Let her go," I said.

The words came out before I could think better of them. Had I been calmer, it would have occurred to me that my interference might well make matters worse. But Mary was family—I knew she was family because of the way my breath shortened and my blood boiled, watching her tremble in the warden's grasp.

Warden Drayton turned on me. His hard grey eyes darkened with further disgust.

Maybe it was because I was Oathbroken. Warden Drayton was the Ivory Warden—a man in the image of Noble Gallant, who'd given us our honour. Broken Oaths were no doubt especially insulting to him. But I knew intuitively that Warden Drayton would never look at Warden Ravenelle the way that he looked at me.

I was, as always, that most loathsome combination of things: an Oathbroken goblin.

"You're hurting her," I said calmly. I knew, all the way down to the roots of my bones, that I was about to take a beating. I didn't care.

I've seen some truly horrifying things in my time. I've seen soldiers kill one another, of course. I once stood on the deck of *HMS Caliban* and watched the Imperium's greatest flagship crash upon the capital city below. I've looked upon the slopes of Pelaeia, everburning with aether, and heard the lingering screams of the ghostly echoes that haunt it.

Warden Drayton might have been a powerful man… but he was nothing compared to my own personal nightmares.

"Warden Drayton." I heard Ravenelle's voice distantly, as though from a long way away. I had forgotten he was even there. "There's no harm done. Let's not distress the young lady."

Cool serenity washed over me, dulling the edges of my anger. Warden Drayton shifted his eyes away from me—no less hateful, but now less urgent. I realised then that I was trembling with the anticipation of violence.

"Trouble, gentlemen?" I heard Warden Albright's voice now, sharp with displeasure. Three of the wardens had gathered once again, drawn by the fallout from Mary's dramatics.

"No trouble," Warden Ravenelle said. A subtle, soothing hum of aether infused his voice. "A bit of excitement, perhaps. Could I borrow your retiring room, Warden Albright?"

"I really think you better," Warden Albright said. "Warden Drayton

—I know you ain't about to get that gob's blood all over my nice clean floors. In the middle of a party, no less."

Warden Albright spoke the words with a dark humour that I didn't share. What sympathy I'd had for her withered somewhat in that moment. I was a *gob*, once again—reduced to an inconvenience, rather than a person. I realised then that I had imagined up a potential bond between us; I'd believed that surely, a woman in her position would intuitively understand a goblin in *my* position.

There was no such bond. There had been no real reason to expect one, except for the fancies of my overactive imagination.

Navi had come around to grab Mary by the shoulder, pulling her out of Warden Drayton's grip with a maternal scowl upon her features. Drayton released her, still staring me down.

"I'm so sorry," Mary whispered to Warden Ravenelle again. Her voice was choked with tears, and I knew this time that they were no act.

Displeased murmurs rippled through the party. The social tides had turned against Warden Drayton for the moment. He narrowed his eyes and whirled to stalk away.

"You *begged* me to come to this party!" Navi scolded Mary. "You swore you would behave, Mariah!"

Navi had somehow managed to keep up her act, in spite of the tension. With steely nerves like that, I thought, she ought to have been an aethermancer.

Mary quailed beneath Navi's lecture, clinging to her hand. Navi sprinkled fervent apologies at the wardens, even as she drew Mary further and further away from them.

Warden Ravenelle paused to speak with Warden Albright—but he glanced my way, just over her shoulder, and our eyes met again.

I dipped my chin at him this time, acknowledging the debt between us.

* * *

"That was a close call," Strahl observed from behind his visor. "I was certain they were going to throw you out."

We'd retreated to the corner of the ballroom closest to Caphea's window, where Mr Strahl waited for us. I didn't immediately see Mr Finch, but my confusion was soon remedied when I caught sight of him just beneath the tablecloth, tinkering with the floating table on his hands and knees. Strahl had angled himself to block Mr Finch from general view as he worked.

I continued playing my servant's role, ushering Mary to a chair. She stared at the wardens on the other side of the room; Warden Ravenelle had excused himself, even as Warden Ferric arrived to satisfy his curiosity.

A few paces away from us, Navi patiently endured Lady Fortinault's chiding suggestions of ways to take Mary in hand.

"Give it time," I told Strahl wryly. "Lady Fortinault is coming up with creative punishments for Mary, even as we speak."

Mary clenched her hands against her knees. "I hate them all," she whispered, between angry tears. "They all think they're so important —like that gives them the right to push people around. I wish I was an aethermancer. I'd duel that stupid warden and embarrass him in front of everyone."

The very idea sent a shiver of horror through my bones. Warden Drayton didn't strike me as the sort to hold back in a duel. "Maybe someday," I told Mary diplomatically. "But we'll certainly get the chance to humiliate the wardens in other ways, tonight."

Mary shot me a dark look. "I bet that lady warden's going to be real embarrassed when we walk out of here with that faerie," she said. "I hope she is. I hope it's awful for her. Serves her right, for what she called you." She paused and sucked in a breath, steadying herself with rage. "And I hope that old Drayton gets warts where the sun doesn't shine. I hope his nose rots and his toes fall off—"

"Let's focus on the job, Mary," I said, though part of me dearly wished to let her keep going. "We don't know how long Warden Ravenelle will be gone. We need to make our move." I glanced surreptitiously beneath the table. "How are we doing down there, Mr Finch?" I asked.

Something sparked beneath the tablecloth, and a muffled curse drifted upwards.

"I am making progress," Mr Finch said primly, "but I'm working with relatively few tools and even less light." His hand popped out from beneath the table, in a beckoning fashion. "Wine," he requested firmly.

I retrieved a single glass of wine from the table, where it had been waiting for him, and pressed it into his hand.

"Thank you," Mr Finch said. Both the hand and the glass disappeared beneath the tablecloth.

Navi nodded one last time at Lady Fortinault and turned back to rejoin us. "Look distressed, will you?" she asked me. "I told Lady Fortinault I would be hiring a governess for Mary and dismissing you from service, effective first thing tomorrow. I couldn't get out of the conversation otherwise."

I didn't have to pretend very hard to put on a tired, miserable expression. Navi shot me a sympathetic look, as she kept her back to the noblewoman behind us.

"All this pettiness," Navi sighed at me. "I feel like I've aged a decade. I can't wait to see the sky again."

"From your lips to the Benefactor's ear," I sighed back. "Thankfully, Mr Finch is well on his way to securing a source of aether for us. All we need to do now is distract the wardens." I paused as I thought of the scene we'd just escaped. "Again, I mean to say. Hopefully in a more explosive and less personal manner."

Navi smiled at me. "Why, that's the easy part, Captain," she said. She glanced over her shoulder at Lord and Lady Fortinault. "I know just who to enlist in our cause, in fact. I'll require you to accompany me—I hope you'll forgive any unpleasantness involved in the matter."

I nodded wearily and glanced back at Mary. She'd worked her way through her anger, and back into grim determination.

"Can you handle keeping a lookout for Warden Ravenelle?" I asked her. "If he comes back too early, it would be useful to have you head him off with crying and apologies."

Mary nodded stiffly. "Yes, Cap'n," she said. The task seemed to focus her again, at least, diverting her for the moment from her wishes for strategically-placed warts.

Lady Navi straightened her back and took a steadying breath. She reached down to adjust my coat, and I saw that her hands had begun to shake very slightly. "We're very near to done," she said. I suspected that the statement was more for her own benefit than for mine.

"We are," I agreed. I shot her a wry smile. "We're acting, Lady Navi," I said. "I don't take it personally, I promise."

Navi sighed heavily. "There was a time when it was not an act," she said softly. "I am able to put on this face because it was once mine in truth. And I am certain that its remnants will always be with me. I may find that woman intolerable... but some part of me still enjoys her admiration."

"Navi," I said. I met her eyes directly. "I wore an Imperial uniform. I sang patriotic songs and made wagers on how long it would take us to crush the North. I *still* have dreams where I'm some improbably decorated war hero." I had to work not to look away. "The awful things we believe in rarely truly disappear. But I like to think we're both better people than we were, at least. And I don't think either of us is ever going back to the way we were before."

The job before me was evidence of that, wasn't it? William the child soldier would have been thrilled to walk among all of these former Imperial nobles—he would have been especially awed by the wardens of Lyonesse and the prospect of a new, heroic empire.

Captain William Blair saw the foolish emptiness of it all... and the danger that new empire represented.

Navi looked down at me with uneasy empathy. "It's not the same, William," she said softly. "You were poor and desperate for opportunities. I had every opportunity in the world."

"I can't afford to let myself off the hook, Navi," I told her. "I don't want... I *can't* go back to the way I used to be." I swallowed and nodded past her shoulder. "I believe we have a heist to complete," I added. "Shall we, Kumari?"

Navi nodded minutely. The haughty noblewoman's mask returned to her face; she turned crisply on her heels and marched back towards Lord and Lady Fortinault. I hurried after her with an appropriately tired expression.

"You should have been keeping a better eye on Mariah," Navi snipped at me. "I expect that sort of behaviour from her—but I pay *you* to keep her in hand."

"Yes, Kumari," I said with a cringe. I tried to look painfully chastised.

"I am *terribly* sorry," Navi said to Lady Fortinault. "Good help is so hard to find these days. You were right, Lady Fortinault—I've allowed Mary to cloud my judgement for too long. She's reaching the age where she requires proper tutelage. William simply cannot fulfil that function."

Lady Fortinault sighed sympathetically at Navi. "Sometimes we must do what is best for our children and not what makes them happy," she said.

It still stung to be talked over as though I wasn't present. But I was Captain William Blair and not William the servant. The contempt might be real, and hurtful… but at least I couldn't lose a job I'd never had in the first place. All I wanted—all I *needed*—was the faerie in the display case.

"This party *was* too excitable for Mary, in the end," Navi said. "I've told her to take some time in the corner, for now. I only hope Warden Ferric issues his challenge soon—it would certainly help everyone to forget about her embarrassing mishap."

Lord Fortinault shot Navi a curious look. "Whatever do you mean, Kumari?" he asked.

Navi blinked. "Oh," she said. "Well, I was certain it was general knowledge by now. Oh dear. I'm not certain it's my place to say."

I turned my body towards the display case, locking my eyes upon the faerie inside of it. The strange, ghostly presence of her will focussed upon me. I brought my hand up to my throat, as though to adjust my cravat, and signed the word: *curiosity*.

Both nobles leaned in towards Navi, scenting the hint of salacious gossip.

"My dear Kumari Varma," Lady Fortinault said sweetly. "You *are* among friends. You can speak freely with us." The noblewoman placed a familiar hand upon Navi's arm.

Navi allowed herself to be swayed. She leaned in conspiratorially. "Well... you'll recall that we discussed Warden Ferric at supper," she said. "I believe you had speculated that he would challenge Warden Albright any day now, Lord Fortinault?"

"I did," Lord Fortinault said. "I have good money wagered that he'll do it sometime this week, in fact."

Navi smiled coyly at him. "I suspect you will have cause to collect on your wager," she said. "I *did* have the opportunity to make my social rounds this evening. After Warden Albright greeted the rest of the wardens so rudely, several people have said that Warden Ferric is bound to issue his challenge *tonight*. He is a man of dignity, after all. You know him better than I do, of course—he would never endure such shame without reply, would he?"

Lord Fortinault raised his eyebrows. "But... in her own home?" he asked. "At her own *party?*" There was a hint of hungry excitement in his voice that suggested he was less than scandalised.

Lady Fortinault let out a soft gasp at the idea.

"He *is* the Scarlet Warden, after all," Navi said, with a rueful smile. "A Fool's fool, one might say—both bold in action and utterly fearless. It could only behoove his reputation to act now. Besides which, Warden Albright all but dared him, did she not? She said he would have to duel her if he wanted a better look at that faerie artefact."

Lord Fortinault nodded urgently. "Of course," he said. "Of *course*. That brazen woman. She clearly doesn't expect anyone to call her bluff."

Navi's smile sharpened. "Albright clearly believes that politeness will stay Warden Ferric's hand tonight. Her arrogance has become dangerous. Why... I heard someone call him a *coward* in her presence."

Navi lowered her voice. "The lady warden did not contradict the description."

Lady Fortinault widened her eyes. "No!" she whispered with excitement. "Surely not!"

Navi shook her head. "I certainly chose the right season to visit Lyonesse," she said. "I was sure that Warden Ferric was simply waiting for the right time to challenge Albright... but I wonder now. Do you think he's realised what people are saying about him? I can't imagine anyone would dare to slander him to his face. But then... who would be brave enough to warn him?"

I glanced meaningfully at the display case again. I had to stay very carefully behind Navi as I signed the next word: *arrogance.*

I saw the change in the two nobles only because I was watching for it. They were already stuffed to the gills on their own self-importance... but that self-importance soon solidified into an impossible assurance.

Faeries, I decided, were even more terrifying than I had imagined them to be.

"Warden Ferric surely deserves to know that his reputation is in danger," Lady Fortinault said.

"Without a doubt," Lord Fortinault agreed sternly. "Those wagging their tongues behind his back are the *true* cowards."

Navi gave Lord Fortinault an uncertain look. "I fear I'm a coward myself," she said. "I thought to tell him, but... well, I've been here for only a few days. I expect such a conversation wouldn't go very well at all."

Lady Fortinault shook her head. "No, of course not, my dear Kumari," she said. "You're entirely correct. The truth should come from someone who is at least familiar to him. Someone he would trust to have his best interests in mind."

Yes, I thought, with a trace of smugness. *That is exactly the point.*

Lord Fortinault straightened, placing his wife's hand upon his arm. "Please excuse us, Kumari," he said. "It seems we have a delicate matter to solve."

Navi had barely nodded her head before the two nobles turned from her to head across the room, angling directly for their target. Warden Ferric, tall and scarlet-clad, was not a difficult man to find.

Navi and I exchanged satisfied smiles and followed in their wake.

6

SECOND OF THE CITY - AN ACCEPTABLE CHALLENGE - FROOFY GOWNS & FIREARMS - PARTY CRASHERS

A sycophantic gaggle of guests already surrounded Warden Ferric. His interest in the other wardens had evaporated in the face of his ardent admirers. By the time we came within earshot, he was already recounting some of his older exploits in Lyonesse's grand arena.

Warden Gordian Ferric was a good foot and a half taller than I was, and another me wider at the shoulders. His armour was *not* ceremonial—it had clearly seen use, according to its scratches and dents. The blade at his hip was large enough to cut me in two, even without the use of aethermancy. It seemed almost unfair that a man so huge should also be blessed with such a potent command of aethermancy.

An overly moon-eyed woman had inched her way quite close to the aethermancer as he spoke. "Lyonesse is so fortunate to have you," she cooed flirtatiously. "The Lady herself must have sent you to our doorstep."

Lord Fortinault and his wife had just made it within earshot of the conversation. The lord straightened his back and plastered a superior scowl upon his features.

"If only everyone here felt the same way," Lord Fortinault declared.

Whatever his other qualities, Lord Fortinault certainly had a well-honed sense of dramatic timing.

A chorus of gasps erupted from the small crowd around Warden Ferric. I might have imagined it, but I thought that a sinister, otherworldly ribbon of outrage flickered through the gathering beneath those gasps. Several of the guests had partaken excessively of the alcohol at this point, and I could only assume that this made them even more susceptible to the faerie's projected emotions.

"Excuse me?" Warden Ferric demanded.

Lord Fortinault wilted slightly beneath the large man's fury—but he continued speaking quickly, intent on absolving himself. "I think very highly of you myself, sir!" Lord Fortinault said. "But others here have been whispering behind your back, and I cannot stand their duplicity any longer."

Tuath bless these bored nobles. Lord Fortinault had garnered exactly the reaction he was after; several of the people nearby now showered him with rapt attention. After everything that had already happened tonight, it was clear that *this* was bound to be the scandal of the evening.

Warden Ferric narrowed his eyes. "And what *precisely* have these others been saying?" he asked Lord Fortinault. Ferric's voice now held a dangerous tone.

"Outrageous things," Lady Fortinault said, from her husband's arm. "Things that no decent person would ever give credit." She pitched her voice to a stage whisper, which still carried all the way over to us. "Warden Albright… she has called you a *coward*, sir."

Several people made shocked noises. One woman dropped her wine glass on the floor.

I had to smother my own manic laughter.

Lady Fortinault hadn't been satisfied with the story we'd told her. In her endless wisdom, she had decided to embellish it *further*.

Warden Ferric tightened his jaw, and I knew that he'd taken the bait.

"You have endured insult after insult from that woman, Warden Ferric," Lady Fortinault lamented. "I know very well that you have done so because you are a gentleman. But truly, the lady warden has shown that she will only take advantage of your impeccable manners."

I turned towards the display case, flashing my hands quickly. *Anger,* I signed to Syrene. I pointed emphatically at Warden Ferric, marking him as her current target.

Fury slammed into the gathering, so quickly that it stole my breath. I blinked back dizziness, struggling to stay upright.

The anger that swept over me was merely collateral damage, however. Most of it had honed in upon the Scarlet Warden. Even as I watched, his face flushed with wrath. We had clearly identified the chink in his mental armour—for even his vaunted aethermancer's will did nothing to restrain those dark emotions.

"I *have* done my best to be a gentleman," Warden Ferric said coldly. "The lady's mentor is dead. She was owed some allowances for her behaviour." He paused, and his face hardened. "But this goes far beyond allowances. I will not allow her to sully my honour—and the honour of the wardens, as well! She is not fit to wear her title. It is far past time someone took it from her."

Lord Fortinault raised his glass in agreement. "To Warden Ferric!" he declared. "Third… no, *Second* of the City!"

Several of the gathered nobles cheered, not to be outdone.

I glanced quickly at the faerie in the display case. *Deserve,* I signed to her. *He deserves this.*

As the small crowd cheered, Warden Ferric's glower morphed slowly into a smug, prideful expression. It was such an ugly sight that I nearly recoiled. But that smugness held a natural place among this particular gathering—it was so ubiquitous and expected that its ugliness was invisible to the people that surrounded me.

Thankfully, no one expected a common goblin servant to cheer.

Warden Ferric downed his wine. He passed off the empty glass to the nearest lady and squared his shoulders. "Please beg my pardon, my lords and ladies," he declared. "I have a duel to win."

The Scarlet Warden turned his attention just across the room, where Warden Albright currently spoke with her own, smaller entourage. The nobles around us parted to let him pass, as he marched in her direction with his head held high.

Navi and I backed away from the crowd, intent on making ourselves scarce. Slowly, we retreated to the corner table, where the rest of the crew still waited.

Mary peered over my shoulder at Warden Ferric, tapping her toe with barely contained glee. "Did it work?" she asked.

I smiled grimly at her. "Lovely night for a duel, isn't it?" I said.

Mary narrowed her eyes with vicious satisfaction. "It sure is," she replied.

I felt one last pang of guilt over the trouble I'd sent in Warden Albright's direction... but that bit of guilt ebbed away as I remembered the ease with which the word *gob* had tripped from her lips.

This gob is taking your faerie and leaving, I thought at her.

I heard the clatter of tools beneath the table.

"How are you faring, Mr Finch?" I asked.

"Quite well, Captain," Finch replied through the tablecloth. "I'm feeling much more relaxed already. I could use another glass of wine though, if you happened to be of a mind—"

I sighed. "How is your *work* faring, Mr Finch?" I corrected myself. "Can you pry out the power source?"

"Oh," Mr Finch said sheepishly. "Yes. I'll have it in another minute or so. But the moment I pull the power source free, the table will cease levitating. I'll await your signal before I remove it."

I smiled with satisfaction. "Splendid," I said.

"Warden Albright!" The booming shout carried across the room, cutting through the din of the party. Warden Gordian Ferric had planted himself just opposite of his ebon counterpart. "Your hospitality is without question," he called out. "Indeed, you make for an excellent hostess."

The party chatter suddenly stopped.

Warden Albright turned to look at the other warden with a confused expression. "Thanks, I guess," she said. "You don't gotta yell it, you know. My ears work just fine." Her voice drifted over the sudden silence in the room.

Navi beckoned the rest of the table to move in closer to listen.

"An excellent hostess—" Warden Ferric declared again. "—but a terrible warden!"

"Hm," Navi mused. "A bit on the nose, isn't it?"

"Good dramatic reveal, though," Mary said.

"Excellent elocution!" Mr Finch noted from beneath the table.

A unified sound of agreement went up among the crew. Even Strahl inclined his head.

Warden Albright's posture stiffened slowly. It was hard to tell from a distance, but I thought I could see a few sparks of pale blue lightning flickering around her clenched fist.

I didn't even have to signal Syrene this time. Warden Albright was humiliated... and *furious*.

"So that's how this is gonna go," Albright said. Her voice was low and deadly.

"You act surprised," Warden Ferric observed. "You allowed your mentor's murderer to escape your grasp. You have confiscated a prize which clearly belongs to the entire city and dared us to challenge your claim to it. But worst by far, Warden Albright, are your *manners*—or lack thereof."

"*That's* the worst part?" I muttered.

"His priorities do seem a bit backwards," Navi said. "The crowd is on his side, though."

It was true. The Ebon Warden's guests had all turned upon her, clearly eager to watch her embarrassment.

The electrical discharge around Warden Albright grew more intense. "Get. *Out*," she snarled at the other warden.

"No," Warden Ferric said. I *felt* his self-righteousness, slimy and uncomfortable against my skin. "I hereby challenge your title, Warden Jasmine Albright. Accept this duel—or yield your status as Second of the City."

Warden Drayton stepped between the two of them. "A challenge has been offered," he observed. He paused, searching the room. I realised he was probably waiting for Warden Ravenelle's interjection… but the man was still neatly indisposed, and nowhere to be found. Warden Drayton cleared his throat and continued. "As Ivory Warden and First of the City, I witness this before Noble Gallant. Warden Albright—what is your response?"

Warden Albright raised her closed fist. Lightning snarled within it, spitting its rage upon the air. The blue veins on her face lit up with sudden incandescence.

"You want a fight?" she said. "You've got one. It sure ain't gonna go the way you seem to think it will, though."

"The Ebon Warden has accepted a challenge from the Scarlet Warden," Drayton noted. "To the winner goes the title of Second of the City." He paused. "Your houses shall need to negotiate the time and place—"

I winced and signed frantically at the display case. *Now!* I begged Syrene. *They need to duel right now!*

A deafening thundercrack cut off Warden Drayton partway.

"No need," Warden Albright spat. "We got a nice patch of ground just outside. Let's get this over with—*now*."

Drayton might have had a response for this—but Warden Ferric interrupted him.

"Now is *ideal*," Ferric bit off coldly.

The two duellists turned on their heels, marching for the ballroom's exit. Warden Drayton hurried belatedly after them, with a bit less dignity than one might have expected from the First of the City.

The eerie silence broke, all at once. A buzz of excitement overtook the ballroom. Guests flooded for the glass doors that led out onto the balcony, all politely jostling for the best position from which to watch the duel. Even the servants crowded in near the back, painfully aware that their brand new employer was about to engage in both political and physical violence.

The two Lyonguard closest to the display case, however, were unswayed.

"Everyone's distracted," I hissed. "Or, well—*most* of them are distracted. Mr Strahl, I hope you can handle the remainder?"

Strahl inclined his head coldly, and started his way towards the two Lyonguard.

"Mr Finch," I said, "I'm going to need that power source."

"Yes indeed!" Mr Finch replied from below. "On the count of three, Captain. One, two—"

Aetheric discharge crackled over the last word, obscuring it. There was a flash from beneath the table, followed by the sharp stench of ozone.

The gleaming light at the centre of the table flickered. It wobbled once—and then, it came crashing down.

I lunged for the table. Navi and Mary followed suit, but none of us were terribly strong. We managed, at least, to redirect the table's fall, just as Mr Finch crawled out from beneath it, dusting off his shirt with a disgruntled-looking expression.

The table hit the floor with a *clang* that sounded far too loud.

I glanced around sharply—but most of the people who might have taken interest in us were currently shouting over the balcony outside.

The only people who looked back our way were the two Lyonguard by the display case. But they had far more pressing concerns.

Strahl was on them the moment they turned their heads our way. He drove an armoured fist into the first man's faceplate, rocking the man back onto his heels; his head slammed back into the display case with a painful crack. As the Lyonguard began to slump, Strahl drew the man's sword from its sheath and spun.

The second Lyonguard was far too slow on the uptake. As his reactions caught up with him, he reached for his own sword—but it was too late. Strahl kicked at the back of the other man's knee, forcing him to kneel. He struck the basket-hilt of the stolen sword neatly across the kneeling guard's face.

He, too, fell to the floor with a clatter.

Strahl lingered over both men just long enough to make certain they were both truly unconscious. I felt, once again, a mixture of awe and discomfort as I considered how little time it had taken him to *handle* two Lyonguard.

"Ahem." Mr Finch cleared his throat, and I glanced sharply at him.

My chief engineer leaned down to drag a leather valise from behind the table. Stashed inside, atop a pile of his usual tools, was a charged crystalline core of pure aether, around the size of my fist. A thin silver shell encased most of the core, but at least a third of the crystalline aether was now fully exposed, where it had once fitted into the table. Slim tubes ran from the shell, no longer attached to any mechanisms. Even as I watched, transparent wisps of blue-white aether evaporated off the sphere, filling the valise with iridescent smoke.

Mr Finch had not entered the party with his valise.

"Where did you get that?" I asked, bewildered.

Mary lifted her hand with a proud smile. "I made my dress for smuggling!" she said. "It's got pockets, too!"

"We should hurry," Mr Finch said anxiously. "Crystalline aether is... *less* volatile, but it's still not healthy to be carrying it around like this."

I politely declined to remind the man that there were four expert aethermancers on site who could do far worse than give us a bit of mild aether poisoning. Instead, I whirled for the centre of the dance floor, where Strahl's armoured figure had just finished dragging the pair of downed Lyonguard out of sight from the balcony.

As I approached Syrene, I felt the edges of a new emotion welling up inside me. *Excitement. Awe. Fascination.*

Lightning flashed outside, highlighting the ballroom in stark white. Thunder cracked, so loud that my ears rang slightly. The crowd on the balcony gasped in excitement, and I realised that their fixation upon the duel was perhaps a bit more intense than it ought to have been.

"Very clever," I addressed the display case, as I came close enough to see the faerie.

I hadn't thought Syrene would be able to hear me through the glass

—but I imagined that I saw her flowers sway in pleased acknowledgement.

Mr Finch came after me, carefully depositing his valise next to the display case. He glanced up at the statue of Tiirdan, still perched upon the case, and sighed.

"It's too tall for me to reach it with just a chair," he said morosely. "I'll need more elevation than that."

I snorted. "I'm not the man you want for elevation," I said.

Mary giggled behind us. "It's sure not going to be me," she said.

"Well, I'm sure I didn't bring this strapping bodyguard for nothing," Navi observed, with a sideways glance at Strahl.

Strahl sighed heavily. "Really?" he asked.

A gout of golden, fiery light lashed across the gardens outside.

"Now would be good," I said urgently. "Just… put him on your shoulders, will you?"

"This is going to be most uncomfortable," Mr Finch groaned.

Strahl felt the urgency of the situation just as keenly as the rest of us. He let out a heavy growl of frustration and kneeled down in front of Finch. "Go on," he said. "Let's get this over with."

Under other circumstances, the sight of my bean pole of an engineer trying to balance himself atop an armoured tin can might have been laughable. Mr Finch had to hold onto Navi and Mary's hands as Strahl surged back to his feet; the older man still wobbled dangerously for a moment, with a soft squeak of alarm.

I'll admit: I still laughed. Quietly.

"There's a panel in the statue," Mr Finch said, in a strained voice. "I can just see it. Move a step to the right, will you?"

Strahl clanked sideways, and Mr Finch caught himself against the statue with another tiny cry.

"Not so fast!" he begged. "I'm barely hanging on. Er—would someone kindly pass me my tools?"

"Just tell me what you need," Mary offered. She couldn't quite keep the grin from her face as she looked up at the engineer.

"Right, I'll—I'll call them out to you," Mr Finch said, with what little dignity he could muster. "But be *very* careful of that core, young woman. I dare say it's the only expensive thing in this room you would regret touching."

"I have no idea what you mean by that," Mary said innocently. She pulled a screwdriver from the valise and flipped it up towards Mr Finch's hand. "The panel up there has screws, doesn't it? You'll probably need this one."

I glanced back towards the balcony with my heart in my throat. The duel was still going, which meant that Warden Albright had so far held her own against Warden Ferric. But regardless of which one eventually came out triumphant, I couldn't imagine that an aethermancy duel would last all *that* long.

"As soon as Syrene's free, we make like the South Wind and storm out of here," I said. "Straight to the roof, everyone—no pausing for silverware, please. You've got our flare, Mary?"

"Yessir!" Mary said. "Hold onto this for Mr Finch, will you?"

She passed me a long tool with a delicate hook. As I took it from her, Mary reached back towards the bustle of her dress. A few moments later, the hoop and bustle both clattered to the floor, revealing a set of practical-looking trousers and two neatly-holstered firearms. Mary turned out the hoop, and I saw that there was an entire bandolier of munitions hidden inside of it. The bustle was, itself, a buttoned-up sort of satchel, from which Mary retrieved a small collection of flares.

"Now then!" Mary proclaimed. "Who wants a weapon?"

I gestured with my empty hand, and Mary unbuttoned one of the holstered guns at her side to pass it over to me, belt and all. Navi fished beneath her own voluminous skirts to retrieve two halves of a shortened, lever-action rifle, which she soon pieced back together.

Mary pulled the other gun from her side and squinted up at our chief engineer. "Mr Finch seems indisposed," she observed. "I'll just hold onto this—"

"*No,*" I said. "Not until you're older, Mary. Give me the revolver."

Mary heaved an incredibly put-upon sigh. "I carried a gun before I ever joined the crew, you know," she said. "It's not like the streets were real friendly, Cap'n—"

"No," I repeated. "That's final, Mary. I don't want you looking like a threat if things go sideways." I buckled the first gun to my side and held out my hand again.

Mary grumbled once more... but she passed the second revolver over to me.

"Do you have my—" I started.

Mary extracted my hatchet from the mess of fabric that had once been her skirt.

"Thank you," I said. I set the second gun aside for Mr Finch, then took the hatchet.

Mary reached down to retrieve her hoop, grumbling to herself as she pieced it back together.

"Would someone *please* pass me my—" Mr Finch started.

I pressed the hook-shaped tool into his hand. He took it with a sniff of indignation.

"Mary," I said, "go scout our exit. Lady Navi—you're with her."

Mary eyed the revolver next to me one last time. I shot her a narrow-eyed look, though, and she turned for one of the ballroom's exits with a sigh. Navi followed swiftly after her, with her rifle held behind her.

"Aha!" Mr Finch exclaimed triumphantly. "Nearly there. Now, Captain—if you could *carefully* hand me the aether core. Only touch the silver, please, if you like your fingers the way they are."

I reached carefully into the valise, obeying his instructions. Even before I touched the shell, I felt the spark of aether against my hand.

It's hard to describe the touch of aether to someone who's never felt it. It isn't hot, and it isn't cold; neither is it wet, for all that it can sometimes look like steam. And though aether often sparks, it's not the same as the feeling you get when you shock yourself in the winter.

What aether *does* feel like is... potential. It's a wild, startling feeling —like flying through a storm cloud, or standing at the edge of a tall precipice.

The ambient aether in the valise sank eagerly into my hand. The bleeding edge of it travelled up my arm, making me feel giddy and powerful. As I closed my fingers around the silver shell, I felt the aether like a bolt to my heart. I swayed drunkenly on my feet.

"Whew," I managed. "That's… *something.*"

"I *did* warn you," Mr Finch sniffed. "Now, pass it up—*carefully!*"

I pressed the core into his hand, silver side first. As I released it, a few lingering sparks flickered against my palm. The drunken, powerful feeling lightened—but it didn't quite disappear.

Mr Finch fiddled with one of the tubes that led away from the silver core, attaching it to something he'd exposed in the statue. Shortly thereafter, I heard an aetheric crackle, and a metallic *ka-CLUNK.* Gears clicked beneath our feet; the thick glass case surrounding the trapped faerie sank into the floor, leaving both the heavy statue and its contents floating eerily in midair.

"Oh thank goodness," Mr Finch breathed. "I wasn't certain that would work." He fumbled briefly with the aetheric core, and I rushed to take it from him, stashing it back within the valise.

"Of course it was going to work," I said. "You are, after all, a genius, Mr Finch."

My engineer puffed up a bit at this, still halfway drunk on aether fumes. He tottered on Mr Strahl's shoulders, however, and the tall, armoured man shifted on his feet in alarm.

"Time to get down," Strahl said. "Hold on for a second, would you?"

Finch blinked and leaned himself against the statue for a moment as Strahl lowered himself back to his knees. I caught the engineer's hands and helped him stumble away from Mr Strahl.

"That was bracing," Mr Finch mumbled. "Very invigorating. Let's not do it again, please, Captain."

I patted him on the shoulder. "Good man!" I told him. "You're done, Mr Finch! Go join the ladies, please. They'll make sure you reach the roof safely."

Mr Finch staggered in the same direction that Navi and Mary had gone, and I returned my attention to the cache of relics before me.

Syrene still floated within, suspended in an invisible aether field. This close, I could just see the hint of a smooth, inhuman face within the wood. She had thin, delicate features—so narrow that they barely registered at all. Her eyes were closed, half-hidden beneath the fall of blooming flowers that was her hair. She looked for all the world as though she were asleep.

"Can she... move?" I asked Strahl uncertainly. I had been hoping that the faerie might spring to life as soon as the display case was opened—but though I felt her alertness against my skin, her eyes did not open.

"Syrene was... badly injured," Strahl said gruffly. "She's still recovering. We'll have to carry her out." He shot me a sideways glance. "She can still navigate."

I let out a breath. "That's not what I was worried about," I said. I turned back to the faerie in question. "Er... terribly sorry. Do you *mind* if I carry you? I don't want to offer insult, my lady."

Time was pressing—but I'd have to be an even greater fool than I was to touch a faerie without asking.

Someone else's warm amusement rippled through me. I took it as a yes.

I reached out to close my fingers gingerly around Syrene's small waist. The wood was softer and warmer than I'd expected—more like skin than bark. Syrene's flowers surrounded me with a heady perfume, nearly as intoxicating as the aether I had touched before.

Amusement turned to weary gratitude. For just a moment, I thought I saw those sleeping eyelids flutter.

A soft breeze tickled at my ear, carrying a whisper upon it.

"Well met," a feminine voice murmured.

I stared at the faerie for a long, spare moment. Logically, I had accepted that the staff in the display case was actually a living being... but until that moment, I hadn't *believed* it in my bones. It was strange and humbling, knowing that I held such a precious life in my hands.

It was also... tiring, for some reason. I blinked heavily, struggling to stay upright. I tried instinctively to catch myself against the display case—but the glass was gone, and I stumbled to my knees instead.

I wasn't the only one affected. Strahl's armour clanked against the marble floor as he sank to his knees with weariness.

At first, I thought the faerie's exhaustion must have been weighing upon us... but even as I drifted off, Syrene surged with alien alarm. The emotion shot through me like lightning, cutting through the weary blanket that had overcome me.

Soft footsteps sounded behind me on the marble.

"This is... unfortunate," Warden Ravenelle observed. I heard real disappointment in his voice. "I can't imagine you masterminded this yourself... William, was it?"

I blinked quickly, reorienting myself in place. The Cerulean Warden's aura of calm had deepened to a pleasant, nearly-suffocating serenity. Syrene's alertness seethed through my veins, pressing back against it—but I knew that if I hadn't been holding onto her, I would already have been asleep. Strahl had clattered to the floor, unmoving.

Warden Ravenelle paused, now standing over me. His shadow blocked out the artificial aether-stars above me. Active aether outlined his eyes in multi-coloured hues. The silver contraption on his hand whirred with effort; the tube beneath his sleeve painted us both with bright blue light.

"Tell me who arranged this theft," he said softly. "You might still escape this with your neck intact."

I nearly laughed at that. The Cerulean Warden might have managed a moment of empathy for me... but even he couldn't bring himself to believe I was in charge of this little heist.

I pretended far more drowsiness than I felt.

"You don't... understand," I mumbled. I slurred the words as badly as I could.

Warden Ravenelle frowned, leaning down towards me. The humming device on his hand eased its efforts somewhat, and I saw Strahl stir just behind me.

"What don't I understand?" the Cerulean Warden asked softly.

I lashed out, closing my fingers around the tube that connected to the aether focus on his hand.

His iridescent eyes widened—just before I yanked the tube free.

Pure, prismatic aether hissed between us. The very edges of it sank into my skin, and my heart raced with frantic giddiness. I surged to my feet, cracking my forehead into the warden's nose. Pain registered dimly within me, as though from far away—but I felt the cartilage give way, and I knew I'd broken the delicate bones there.

The aura of calm fell away, as though it had never been. At that moment, I realised just how hard Syrene had been working to keep it at bay—for the furious alarm inside me exploded outwards, slamming into every living being in our vicinity.

That wave of emotion reached the duellists outside.

A moment later, a shrieking sphere of aetheric flame flew over the crowd on the balcony, detonating against the tall windows. Every one of them blew inward, in a violent shower of glass.

Guests screamed and fled the balcony. A small stampede of nobility retreated into the ballroom, cringing away from the duel below.

Warden Ravenelle staggered back, clutching at his nose. I didn't envy him—I knew how badly a blow like that could stun a man. I also knew I should take the window of opportunity to run; things were only going to get worse from here on out. But Strahl had yet to reach his feet, and the same impulsive part of me that couldn't leave Evie behind sent me running towards him.

"On your feet, let's go!" I hissed. I tried to haul him up to his feet with my one free hand, but it was no use—his armour was far too heavy.

Strahl groaned. *At least he's waking up,* I thought. If he could only get himself standing, we might yet have a chance—

A violent blast of electric aether boomed outside; this time, it propelled an armoured figure through the broken windows like a cannonball. Guests shrieked and tried to dodge as Warden Ferric shot across the floor. Armour squealed against marble, grating on my ears.

Warden Albright's whip lashed around the railing of the balcony, yanking her upwards in a crack of aether. Like a dark storm cloud, she advanced upon Warden Ferric's struggling form, briefly indifferent to the people near the display case.

Warden Drayton's pale form bolted up the stairs from the garden with a quickness I wouldn't have expected.

"That is *enough!*" Drayton thundered. "This duel is over, both of you!"

"Is that right?" Warden Albright howled back. "You want to stop the duel now that your dog's been whipped, Drayton? You think I don't know what you're up to, you sonuva—"

Albright's slim form halted abruptly. Her eyes locked upon me… and I knew I'd waited too long.

Warden Ravenelle stumbled behind me—still shaky and nauseous from pain, but fully capable of cutting me off from the exit. Blood dripped between his fingers where he held his nose, and I knew there would be no further mercy from that quarter. Warden Ferric groaned and pushed to his feet, blinking away his confusion.

I clutched at Syrene, fully aware that the Lady of Fools had stopped answering my prayers.

All four of Lyonesse's chief defenders and most powerful aethermancers stared at me—a thief on display, with nowhere to hide.

7

WARRING WARDENS - THUNDERSTRUCK - FAMILIAR FACES - A HOUSE DIVIDED

There's no such thing as a *good* thing to say when you're caught red-handed.

"Uh," I stammered. My mind was blank; my heart hammered in my throat. "Now, I know what this looks like."

Warden Ferric swayed on his feet, venting aether from his armour. Warden Ravenelle stared me down icily, still bleeding from his broken nose. Warden Albright's face slowly darkened to a murderous cloud.

Warden Drayton smiled coldly. "Do you still object to a bit of goblin blood on your floors?" he asked Albright archly.

That hateful, condescending tone broke through the haze of panic that had seized me… and suddenly, I knew exactly what to say.

"Don't kill me, please, sir!" I wailed. I threw myself to my knees, holding Syrene out before me in Drayton's direction. "I only did as you asked! It's not my fault the other warden came back!"

I could have kicked Warden Drayton in the nethers and received a less stricken expression.

Three other aethermancers turned their gazes to the flabbergasted Ivory Warden.

"A little help, Syrene," I whispered pleadingly.

A soft wind rose around me, drifting through the flowers of

Syrene's hair. This close to her, I felt it like an exhalation—a vicious, intangible sense of suspicion.

Warden Albright breathed it in deeply, perfectly unaware of the manipulation. She shook her head at Drayton in slow, furious astonishment. "Well… ain't that just the cherry on top," she said.

Warden Ferric's face turned guarded. "I expected better from a man of Noble Gallant," he said.

"I…" Warden Drayton stammered, suddenly even more ashen than before. "He's lying! *Obviously*, he's lying!"

The air of suspicion deepened. Even Warden Ravenelle looked sceptical now. I remembered belatedly that I had broken the focus he'd been using to keep things calm; he was now fully vulnerable to Syrene's emotional suggestions.

Still, the Cerulean Warden took in a deep breath and steadied himself.

"This has all got a bit out of hand," Ravenelle said carefully. "Clearly, we have some serious matters to discuss—"

"Don't let him kill me!" I cried at Warden Albright. "I'll talk, I'll tell you everything! He told me to play a prank on Warden Ravenelle with Mary, to get rid of him; he said he'd set up the duel so you'd be distracted—"

"He *what?*" Warden Ferric demanded. He whirled on the Ivory Warden. "I agreed to challenge the lady, Drayton, but I never agreed to be part of some common *theft!*"

"He's *lying!*" Warden Drayton repeated. His voice rose now, slightly shrill on the words. "You can't possibly believe this!"

"And why not?" Warden Albright challenged him. "Why *shouldn't* we believe you'd do somethin' like this, you little white weasel? Everyone here knows you got a yellow belly underneath that cape."

The air darkened with black anger now; I heard it on the breeze, tickling at my heart. I hoped, suddenly, that all four of those awful wardens would kill each other. I wanted to see them bleed out on the floor, wailing for mercy. I thought how amusing it would be to see the confusion on their faces, as they realised the terrible joke that had been played upon them—

No.

I choked back that alien hate, shuddering with the effort. It was harder than it should have been; Syrene's inhuman fury thudded against my skin like a heartbeat, soaking into my soul. But I'd indulged that sort of hatred one time too many; I'd seen the ultimate destination at the end of that awful road.

I didn't resist Syrene's hatred because I was a good person. I resisted it because I had been a very *thoughtless* person, once upon a time. As a selfish, short-sighted child, I had burned myself upon that easy hatred; the stark, unavoidable consequences of those decisions still haunted my nightmares. As Syrene seethed in my hands, the scars of my old hatred throbbed in knee-jerk warning.

Warden Albright did not have those scars.

"Let's see you cower, weasel," the Ebon Warden hissed.

Aether hummed. Electricity crawled along Albright's ashen sleeves, spitting with renewed fury. She slashed her hand towards Drayton—and a violent bolt of lightning screeched in his direction.

Warden Drayton threw up his arms. A hemisphere of glass-like aether formed around him; the bolt of lightning cracked against it, and then glanced away towards the ceiling. False stars shattered, raining down upon us like meteors.

"This is *absurd!*" Warden Drayton snarled. Blue-white aether roiled along his arms, forming into thin, translucent lances of power. He hurled the first lance at Warden Albright—just as Warden Ravenelle leapt in his way.

The Cerulean Warden flared with a hazy blue aura; he snatched at the aetheric lance, twisting it out of the air. The translucent shape *dissolved* between his fingers, breaking apart into shimmering aetheric steam.

"Stand down, all of you!" Ravenelle yelled. "There are bystanders here!"

Warden Drayton curled his lip. "Tell that to *her!*" he snarled.

Aether flared between them; tiny shards of half-formed aether blades showered around me, and I threw myself to the floor.

Guests scattered once again. Fresh screams went up among them

—and some tiny part of me *enjoyed* it. They deserved it, all of them, for staring at me like a flower on display—

Tuath preserve me, I needed to get Syrene *out* of that ballroom.

Never mind the new empire she might represent; I knew in that moment that if I didn't remove Syrene from the premises, she would get people killed—right here and now.

"Get up, *now!*" I said to Strahl. I hauled at his arm, tugging fruitlessly at his heavily-armoured figure. Finally, he seemed to regain his senses; he surged upwards with a groan of effort, clambering back to his feet.

"Let's go!" I told him. "While they're—"

"Halt, you thief!" Warden Ferric's voice boomed out from behind us.

"—distracted," I groaned.

I spun around to see Warden Ferric bearing down upon us. He ate up the open ground between us with far too much speed for a man of his size. His sword was still in his hand; the long blade's edges glowed white-hot, as though it had been pulled fresh from a forge.

"Surrender now, or forfeit your lives!" Warden Ferric called out.

Strahl didn't reply. Instead, he whirled upon the warden, swinging the sword he had pilfered from the fallen Lyonguard.

Warden Ferric raised his white-hot blade; the weapons clashed in a shower of sparks. The two men were equally matched in height and mass—both heavily armoured, and both clearly used to overbearing their opponents in a fight. Unfortunately, while Strahl's stolen blade was well-made, it clearly wasn't up to the task of holding off the Scarlet Warden's molten-hot weapon. Strahl's sword glowed with warning, already damaged from its brush with Ferric's blade.

The Scarlet Warden had one disadvantage that Strahl did not, however: he had attended the party without a helmet.

Strahl swung at Ferric again, with unrelenting ferocity. This time, as the warden parried the blow, Strahl followed it up with a merciless punch. Warden Ferric pulled back quickly, with a surprised oath—but Strahl's gauntleted fist still caught his cheek in a glancing blow. It was enough to open a bloody gash across the warden's face.

Ferric staggered beneath the punch, wavering on his feet. But even as he did, he brought his other hand up in a warding gesture, gathering fire within his palm.

Strahl batted the other man's arm wide, just before the gout of flame went off.

The fire caught an empty table to my left; chairs and plates shattered, with strangely-pitched popping noises. I threw my arm in front of my face and ducked behind another table, wincing as a few shards sliced at my hands and sleeves.

Unfortunately, my attire was far from the only casualty. The table that Ferric had hit gave a harsh *snap*, as the aether inside it reacted. Light flashed—and then, with a final *crack*, the entirety of the glass table wrenched from its mooring in the floor, rocketing past me like a bullet. The metallic disk arched through the air, tumbling end over end...

...directly towards Warden Ravenelle.

The Cerulean Warden had diverted himself to safely evacuate guests. The glass table hurtled towards his back, even as he shoved Lord and Lady Fortinault towards an exit.

If I had taken the time to consider my decision at all, I probably would have been too late. But I rarely think too hard in the moment. I'm told it's both my best and my worst quality.

Even as the table started past me, I sprinted for the Cerulean Warden.

I'm not a very heavy man—but I do have a certain instinctive understanding of leverage. I launched myself at Ravenelle's legs in a full dive, taking him down at the knees. We tumbled to the ground in a rolling heap.

The table soared over our heads—and shattered against the wall.

Ravenelle shoved me away with a groan. He rolled painfully onto his hands and knees, and I saw that he'd taken a knock to the forehead; a small cut there already bled profusely, dripping into his eyes.

I winced. It was still probably better than the table would have done to him.

Warden Ravenelle met my eyes with a dazed look.

"There," I managed. "We're even now."

"You do realise I can't let you go," Ravenelle slurred warningly.

I winced. "For what it's worth," I said, "I'm incredibly sorry about this."

Warden Ravenelle blinked—a moment before I rabbit-punched him in his broken nose.

The warden collapsed once more, rolling in pain. I scrambled to my feet, searching the area around us. Thankfully, I had dropped Syrene near the end of my dive; I only needed a few seconds to snatch her up from the floor before I turned back towards Strahl and Ferric.

The two men had locked blades again, slamming together in a tangle of arms and armour. Warden Ferric's sword gleamed like golden sunlight, casting a fiery glow upon them both. Strahl's stolen weapon was dangerously ragged—probably only moments from snapping—but he didn't dare discard it.

I skittered around the edges of that fiery light, careful not to draw attention to myself.

"You should have surrendered," Warden Ferric spat at Strahl. The forge-hot edge of his sword had now melted halfway through the other blade.

"Maybe so," Strahl gritted out. "Wouldn't be the biggest mistake I've made."

Strahl's sword sheared in two, a few inches above the crossguard. He threw himself backwards—but Warden Ferric's red-hot blade caught dangerously against his helmet. The metal heated and twisted. Strahl landed heavily, shoving the helmet off with a sharp gasp of pain.

Warden Ferric raised his sword for a deadly stroke.

I slammed Syrene across the back of his skull.

A few ragged flowers drifted to the floor.

"I'm so sorry," I babbled at the faerie. "I hope you're all right, I didn't mean to hurt you."

My only reply was a deep, wicked surge of satisfaction.

Warden Ferric staggered, clutching at the back of his head. He turned towards me, raising his red-hot sword in a dazed, drunken sort of way.

So… I swung again.

Syrene caught him just under the chin. I heard a *crack* that might have signified a broken jaw.

Warden Ferric faltered—and finally crumpled to the ground. His sword clattered to the floor next to him, neatly snuffed out.

Strahl pushed back to his feet. His eerie white hair and angular features were now fully visible in the false starlight of the room. He shot Warden Ferric a last, grim look before jerking his chin towards the exit.

I didn't need the gesture. I was excessively tired of this party.

A faint light called to us from the open doorway, held aloft at about the height one would expect from a twelve-year-old girl. I could just make out a few of the garish-coloured bows that clung to Mary's hair.

I hiked Syrene beneath my arm. Out of the corner of my eye, I saw Strahl pluck the Scarlet Warden's sword from the floor.

The way was clear. This time, we reached the tall, open door in short order. Mary grinned at me breathlessly, holding up a stolen aether-lantern that looked as though it had been wrenched from the wall.

"The way is clear, Captain!" she said. "We're going out the servants' exit!"

The hallway just past us was better-lit than the ballroom, but it was still a bit murky. My sensitive goblin eyes picked out Navi's figure at the end of the corridor, standing on guard with her rifle. Mr Finch was missing—but I could see his leftover handiwork. A control box in the wall stood wide open, with its innards exposed. Tiny aether tubes had been tangled and reworked; a servants' door just next to the box stood open.

Mary scampered down the corridor towards Navi, signalling her back from her watch point. Guards shouted from the ballroom behind us, but we ignored them, ducking quickly through the side door.

Navi came last, facing the hallway as she backed inside. The guards shouted again—their voices were closer this time—and her rifle cracked. The sound echoed down the corridor.

"We should move quickly," Navi said. "I'm keeping them on their toes, but we'll be in a spot of trouble if they rush us all at once."

Thankfully, the servants' passageway was short; it led straight into a kitchen, where the evening's grand meals had been prepared. The serving staff, smarter than the guests, had long since vacated—which made the kitchen's sole occupant that much more obvious.

Mr Finch stood next to one of the long counters inside. He had in front of him a partially-carved pineapple; one small, yellow chunk stood at the end of an expensive fork, halfway to his mouth.

I shot him a disbelieving look. Gunfire sounded again, and my engineer flinched.

"I… I needed to know!" Mr Finch said defensively.

Navi backed through the door, firing steadily. I grabbed Mr Finch by the shoulder, dragging him with us. He cried out mournfully as the fork fell to the floor.

"This way!" Mary said. She pointed at a wide staircase. "Servants' stairs—they'll get us to the upper floors. Haven't scouted there yet."

I nodded and pulled my pistol from my coat. Strahl and I would have to clear the way.

"Mary, Mr Finch—" I started an order, but cut myself off in surprise as I turned to face them. Mary had shimmied out of her skirt once again, turning it into a sack; she hoisted the makeshift bag over her shoulder with a muffled clatter. Mr Finch clutched frantically at a bulging, tied-up tablecloth.

"Do you mind?" I demanded. "We're in a hurry!"

"Yes, let's hurry!" Mr Finch agreed hastily. He bolted after me, still hauling his tablecloth full of illicit goods. Mary came behind him, hot on his heels. Cutlery rattled in the bundle over her shoulder.

I let out a frustrated sigh and shoved my way towards the stairs.

"Aethermancers!" Navi called. She skittered back from the doorway, firing another warning shot into the hallway. The first Lyonguard came into view with his sword drawn, and with a large shield of aether glowing in his off-hand.

I levelled my revolver and fired—not at the guard, but at a large bag of flour on the shelf by the door.

The bag exploded in a snowstorm of fine powder. Guards coughed and spat as we backed up the stairs. It was a narrow, claustrophobic staircase; I nearly turned an ankle on it before we made it to the top.

"Even the stairs are trying to kill me," I grumbled, as we tumbled through the servants' door upstairs.

Mary poked her head just past me, scanning the hallway. "That way!" she said, pointing with her free hand. I followed the gesture with my eyes and spied two great glass doors leading to the roof above the ballroom—a lovely terrace, overlooking the entire estate.

That would do nicely.

We ran for the doors; Navi had just started to huff and puff next to Mr Finch as we reached them. A pair of ghostly-looking guards stumbled up after us, festooned in pale flour and coughing their lungs out. I fired my pistol at the doorway above their heads, forcing them to duck for cover.

The glass doors gave way to crisp evening air. Elaborate topiaries decorated the rooftop terrace beyond; dainty aetheric lanterns swung on chains, painting the area in a soft blue glow beneath the very real stars above. Tables and chairs had been set out for the most important, exclusive guests, but most of the area was open space.

Said guests—and several liveried servants—huddled off to the side, cowering. Our armed arrival did little to reassure them. Mary drew forth a wide, snub-nosed flare gun, aiming it straight into the air. A bright comet of pale light rocketed into the skies. A few guests screamed, but their frantic cries were lost in the flare's explosion.

"We need somewhere nice and open!" I called back. Dougal would have trouble extracting us from this mess of people and furniture. I narrowed my eyes at a distant stretch of rooftop. "There! Let's go!"

Thankfully, the guests on the rooftop seemed more interested in their own safety than they were in our escape. No one moved to stop us as we hurried across the terrace with our respective pineapples, silverware, and stolen faeries.

The flour-covered Lyonguard arrived behind us—and were shortly mobbed by terrified nobles.

"Get me out of here, this instant!" one matronly woman demanded.

"Do you know who I *am?*" the man next to her said. "I probably pay your salary!"

A few of the arriving Lyonguard peeled off to evacuate the nobles —but others began fanning out to follow us.

Rot and ruin, Dougal needed to get here quickly.

I heard the not-too-distant sound of a roaring engine drawing closer. We were nearly to the flattest stretch of open space—

A blinding bolt of lightning split the night air.

Strahl screamed next to me, clattering to the ground. I stumbled, furiously blinking spots from my sensitive eyes.

As my vision returned, I saw Warden Albright's dark figure standing several paces behind us. Her eyes were bright; her foci still crackled with power. She held her hand outstretched in our direction, with her fingers limned in lightning.

"That's far enough," the Ebon Warden snarled.

Warden Albright was an ashen summer storm.

Her once-sable attire had bleached with streaks of smoky grey; the sleeves of her coat, beneath her metallic foci, were now that ugly dishwater grey that most people associated with aethermancers. Wisps of hair had freed themselves from the tight fighting braid at the back of her head, floating on a spectral breeze. The air around her was choked with buzzing aether; its presence made the air around us drop with pressure.

Her eyes glowed so brightly that, for a moment, I thought they were stars.

Strahl pushed himself back onto his hands and knees, trembling—I didn't want to imagine the burns he had beneath that armour, but somehow, he was still moving. Navi shoved Mary behind her, holding her rifle in one hand.

I stepped—very slowly and very carefully—between the warden and my crew.

I kept my hands in the air, where she could see them; one of those hands was empty, while the other awkwardly clutched at Syrene. To my surprise, I was *not* instantly turned into a sooty, Blair-shaped smear on the rooftop. That was... mildly promising.

"You're that goblin that shoulda been executed," Warden Albright said, in a calm, deadly tone. The air crackled around her as she spoke, as though to punctuate the statement.

"I'm the goblin that *shouldn't* have been executed," I corrected her. "Case of mistaken identity. I remedied the situation myself, since your militia weren't inclined to listen." I paused. "Tell me the truth. You only recognise me because you see *him* now." I jerked my chin towards Strahl, still on his hands and knees behind me.

Warden Albright narrowed those bright eyes. I realised then why she *hadn't* immediately smeared me across the roof.

She was worried about destroying the faerie artefact in my hand.

"Return that staff, *now*," Warden Albright ordered.

Syrene's wild fury surged against my skin. I sucked in a deep, shaky breath. "It doesn't belong to you," I said.

"That wasn't a suggestion," Albright retorted coldly.

It took everything I had just to keep Syrene's ugly anger at bay. I forced a measure of calm into my voice that I did not feel at all. "More importantly," I said slowly, "the staff doesn't *want* to be here."

Warden Albright paused. The lightning in her eyes flickered with doubt.

She believes that, I realised. *She can feel it.*

"By the midnight hour." Warden Ravenelle's voice sounded from behind Albright. "You're *alive*."

Warden Ravenelle was somehow even paler than Albright. His powder blue coat had bleached grey, but the moonlight made it seem nearly white; his silver hair gleamed strangely, lit by his foci from below. He walked behind Albright without worry, like an eye of calm in her storm. Wisps of aether escaped his lips as he exhaled, as though he had gone walking on a chill evening.

His eyes were fixed upon Strahl.

Strahl staggered slowly to his feet. I knew he had to be barely standing, but he managed to make the movement look menacing, all the same.

Albright turned her head slightly, considering the Cerulean Warden. "You know him?" she growled.

Warden Ravenelle stared at Strahl, wordless. I saw in his features a strange mixture of horror, wistfulness, and revulsion.

Strahl shook his head wearily. "I just want to leave, and be left alone," he said.

Warden Albright laughed harshly. "You should've thought about that before you killed Warden Clovis," she said.

Warden Ravenelle shook his head slowly. "You... *you* killed Clovis?" he asked. "Why? Because he broke his Oath?"

Strahl smiled grimly. "If I killed every Oathbreaker in the army," he answered, "I'd never get any rest." He paused. "Clovis wanted to resurrect the Imperium. He was... talking to people. I don't know who. People he believed could make it happen. He wanted my help."

Warden Ravenelle closed his eyes, stricken.

"You didn't know?" Strahl asked. "Guess it's not all the wardens in Lyonesse, after all."

Ravenelle whirled on Albright. "Did you know?" he demanded. His voice carried an uncharacteristic snarl. "Did you *know* Clovis was going to drag us into this?"

Warden Albright started at Ravenelle's explosive tone. Her expression darkened soon after. "I don't owe you explanations any more than the rest of the wardens, you spineless fence-sitter!" she snapped. "I've only had this position a few weeks runnin', an' *every* single one of you has made it miserable! If you want answers from me in my own house, you'll find some of that politeness you always show the *male* wardens."

Ravenelle blinked. I watched as a sense of shamed self-awareness flickered across his features. He took a breath.

"Apologies, Warden Albright," he managed. His tone was now somewhat more respectful, though he kept a wary eye on Strahl. "Did... did you know that Warden Clovis wanted a new Imperium?"

Warden Albright laughed bitterly. "*Everyone* knew Clovis wanted a new Imperium," she said. "The old man wouldn't shut up about it." She shook her head. "I didn't believe he was gonna get one, though. If Clovis was talkin' to someone about it, then I sure wasn't invited to those meetings."

Strahl spat at the roof. "We all know who *was* at those meetings, though... don't we?" He levelled a dark look at Warden Ravenelle. "Drayton is still a power-hungry rat. Why should he settle for ruling a city when he could help rule an empire?"

"No one asked your opinion," Warden Albright snapped at Strahl. Lightning snarled around her hand again in abrupt warning.

"This staff is a symbol of the empire!" I said quickly. I held Syrene before me, keenly aware that Albright wouldn't attack me while I held the faerie. "If it stays here, you'll be dragged into a civil war. And this staff—it *really* doesn't like you. It's brought the wardens to blows once already." I looked Warden Albright in the eyes. "Let it go. Let *us* go. We'll take it far away, and we'll never come back."

Warden Albright's eyes hardened. "An' let some goblin get the best of me twice?" she said. "I ain't gonna turn myself into a laughin' stock on your say-so, gob."

The slur stung, no matter how much I tried not to let it show. The answer didn't—but only because I halfway expected it.

I turned on Ravenelle instead.

"Neither one of us wants another civil war," I said to him. "I know that. I *know* why you broke your Oath of service." I allowed a raw note into my voice. "I saw Pelaeia. I made promises on the slopes of that mountain—more important than any Oath. I swore I'd never let something like that happen again."

The words hit their mark. I saw Ravenelle flinch beneath their weight... and I knew I'd guessed correctly.

The other wardens might have deserted for their own reasons—but Warden Ravenelle had deserted after Pelaeia. It wasn't our broken Oaths that connected us; it was our guilt.

"Let them go," Warden Ravenelle said softly. Albright shot him an incredulous look, and he added, softly: "Please. They can't stay here. This... *can't* happen."

Warden Albright stared at me for a long moment. I saw the struggle on her face as she weighed her personal humiliation against the pleading in Ravenelle's voice. I wanted to scream at her, to beg her to understand how serious this all was—I wanted to tell her what it was like being dragged into a war against your fellow countrymen, to warn her just how hideously she would suffer.

Instead, I said nothing—and it was the hardest thing that I had ever said. I knew that none of my words could move her. I had begged Ravenelle instead, because I knew that she would listen to him—a human, and a warden whose respect she actually craved.

Raised voices came from the estate behind the wardens, as more Lyonguard arrived. Soon, I knew, the last two wardens would be upon us… and maybe one of them would recognise the man I was supposed to call Strahl.

Thankfully, the sound of an approaching longboat's engines droned even closer behind me.

Warden Albright knew she was running out of time, too. She glanced once behind her… then hissed out her breath between her teeth.

"Go," Albright snarled. "Get outta here. An' I never want to see any of you in this city again—am I clear?"

"Crystal clear, ma'am," I breathed. I glanced at Mary and Navi. "Flag him down!"

Mary fumbled through her skirts for a handheld torch. She flicked the aether-powered light in the general direction of our longboat, until the beam caught its inky blotch against the starry night sky. Mr Finch inched further backward, warily hefting his tablecloth of stolen goods.

"Drayton will never let me hear the end of this," Warden Albright said calmly. "I've let Clovis' killer escape *twice*. He'll question my fitness as a warden."

"You didn't let anyone escape," Warden Ravenelle told her. "I rushed in foolishly. You chose to save my life, rather than the artefact."

Warden Albright snorted. "What a hero I am," she scoffed. But I saw a bone-deep relief flicker across her face, even as the light within her foci puttered out into the darkness.

Our longboat pulled up, sidling along the edge of the building. Dougal's familiar figure waited for us in the pilot's seat, with his goggles over his eyes and his Coalition kerchief wrapped about his throat. He leaned over the edge to help Lady Navi aboard.

Mr Finch hurried for the longboat with his armful of loot—but I fixed him with a stern look. *Drop it,* I mouthed. *Now.*

We were already stealing Warden Albright's faerie artefact. We didn't need to add insult to injury.

Mr Finch shot me an imploring look. I raised both of my eyebrows at him.

Very glumly, my chief engineer set the sack down on the roof and hurried aboard the vessel. One lonely, spiky pineapple frond peeked out of the bulging sack.

"Mary," I said. "Three books. *No silverware.*"

Mary heaved a very heavy, put-upon sigh—but she obediently overturned her makeshift bag. Several flashes of silver tumbled into the topiary next to her, before she headed after Mr Finch.

Strahl clambered painfully towards the boat. I had to jump in and set Syrene aside in order to help him up.

"So," Dougal said conversationally, "how was the party?"

"About what you'd expect," I said with a shrug.

"Loads ae powdered wigs and wine?" Dougal guessed.

"Lots of awful people with very proper manners," Mary grumbled, as the longboat began its hasty departure.

"And far too much rouge," Navi sniffed indignantly. She perched herself daintily at the edge of one of the seats, with her rifle next to her legs.

Mr Finch sighed morosely. "I never did get to try that pineapple," he lamented.

"Well..." Mary smiled sheepishly. She sifted through the bundle of fabric that had once been her skirt—and then, she drew out a single, spiky yellow fruit.

Mr Finch blinked owlishly. His eyes misted abruptly, and his pinched-looking face took on a deeply touched expression that I had never seen before.

"Oh," he sighed. "Is… is that for me?"

Mary proudly plopped the pineapple in the engineer's lap.

"It's for you," she said. "But… you have to be less grumpy. At least for a little bit."

Navi tried (and failed) to cover her sudden bark of laughter behind her hand. I fixed Mary with a disapproving glower—but the expression dissolved in short order. It was very hard to be upset at such an oddly touching gesture.

As we returned to the *Rose*, I shook my head, idly wondering if there *was* a market for pineapple piracy.

8

AIRSHIP, SWEET AIRSHIP - ECHOES OF THE IMPERIUM - INTRODUCTIONS - A PRICELESS GIFT

My feet hit the familiar deck—and all at once, my body relaxed in relief.

Clothes aside, I was a captain again.

Dougal swiftly secured the longboat, behind me. Little—ever the diligent first mate—had long since readied the ship for takeoff. Crew scattered for their respective duties, while Holloway accompanied Strahl back to the infirmary. I left Little in charge for just a little bit longer, while I headed to my quarters to shed the servant's uniform I was wearing.

As I pulled back on my captain's coat and slid my battered tricorne back onto my head, I felt... more or less like myself. For all that the servant's uniform had made me nearly invisible, it had also come with a subtle weight—and I was dearly glad to be rid of it.

I stepped back on deck, allowing myself to savour the crew's respectful nods and murmurs of 'Captain' as I strode for the wheel.

Little stepped neatly aside, allowing me the wheel with a wide grin. The entire ship had a giddy sort of energy, born of the shared understanding that we had once again accomplished the impossible.

The wheel felt good beneath my hands.

"Mr Strahl will require a hammock of his own," I told my first

121

mate. "Though, on that note—I'll want to speak with him as soon as Holloway clears him to leave the infirmary."

And the navigator he promised? Little inquired. *I take it you didn't find her?*

I let out a slow breath. "Mr Strahl... did deliver on his promise," I said. "We'll be having an officer's meeting tomorrow. I'll explain more then."

Little's eyebrows inched upwards with curiosity—but he gave a slow nod, rather than pressing me further.

I'll go make arrangements, Little signed. He gave me a casual, two-fingered salute and left me to the meditative comfort of the wheel, beneath a beautiful night sky.

I used the time to consider my upcoming conversation with Strahl.

We had indeed earned ourselves the most unique navigator in all of Avalon—but Syrene came with even more strings attached than I could have possibly imagined. What's more, I was now absolutely certain that Strahl had been a high-ranking officer within the Imperium... and probably guilty of far worse things than anyone else on board my ship.

I wasn't at all sure of the moral implications of keeping them both on my crew. But, one way or another, I was the person that had to make that decision.

Syrene was... deeply troubling. But twice now, Strahl had risked his life to prevent history from repeating. I had always said that the only rule on my ship was agreement that the Imperium should have fallen. Whatever terrible things Strahl had once done in the name of the emperor, I couldn't help a certain sense of relief, knowing that someone else in this world felt as strongly about the matter as I did.

I needed answers, I decided. Not all of them... but more than I currently had, at least.

Well past midnight, I heard Strahl's heavy footfalls heading up towards the quarterdeck. He wore a loose-collared shirt with Rustland stitching—probably borrowed from Little. The two men shared a similar stature, but Strahl's leaner arms forced him to roll the shirtsleeves up to his elbows. His pale scars stood out sharply in the moonlight.

Mr Strahl stopped in front of me, clasping his wrists behind his back. I caught a whiff of medicinal ointment from him, where Holloway had treated his aether-burns.

"You wanted to speak with me?" Strahl asked. He paused for a moment, and then added a clumsy: "Sir?"

The word didn't quite fit on his lips. But I appreciated the early effort.

"That depends," I said. "Are you about to fall over?"

Strahl shrugged painfully. "Plenty of time to rest when I'm dead," he observed. "What did you need from me?"

I mulled my words silently.

"I'm not going to ask who you were, before this," I said finally. "But you were... someone important, weren't you? Ravenelle recognised you."

Strahl grimaced. "I'm not going to pretend otherwise," he said. "I did a lot of very bad things, Captain. Killed a lot of people. I believed, at the time..." He shook his head. "It doesn't matter what I believed."

I stared at the clouds ahead. I heard, in his voice, the echo of an awful sentiment I had felt so many times before. I had long since realised that you couldn't undo the past, no matter how much you wished you could. But laying down to die was hardly a viable answer, either.

Selfish or not—we both wanted to keep living. There were plenty of ways out for those whose shame eclipsed their desire to survive.

I cleared my throat. "Those people Clovis was meeting, behind closed doors... the people talking about bringing back the Imperium. All of it has me worried. Do you think Clovis dying has done anything to undermine those talks?"

Strahl's normally-inscrutable features took on an uneasy expression. "Hard to say," he replied. "I will say... that I expect Ravenelle to start cleaning house, in Lyonesse. He may not succeed—but he's got a better chance at pulling it off with me and Syrene safely gone."

I forced myself to digest the words. I didn't like them. It surprised me how little I liked them, in fact. I felt trapped—terrified by the knowledge that the best thing I could do to prevent an awful future was to run away.

But... I wasn't an all-powerful aethermancer.

I was just one Oathbroken man, with a crew of widows, orphans, and outright criminals. Tonight, we had done our part to stave off disaster. By necessity, someone else was going to have to take their turn.

I nodded half-heartedly at Strahl. "Welcome to the crew, Mr Strahl," I said. "We're headed far from Lyonesse, just as you hoped. Get your rest tonight; I'll introduce you and Syrene to the crew tomorrow." I managed a wry smile. "By the way... how do you take your pineapple?"

* * *

I DISCOVERED the next day that my crew had declared the officer's meeting to be an unusually posh affair.

Little and Evie showed up in their best neckcloths. Miss Brighton appeared wearing the tiniest hat I had ever seen, with a flower casually slipped into her bandolier among the bullets. Dougal sported his kilt, while Holloway wore a dignified (if outdated) waistcoat. If Mr Finch had changed a thing about his clothing, however, I really couldn't tell the difference.

We all watched with bated breath as Mr Finch cut open the pineapple. As the knife cleared the fruit, Lady Navi led the crew in a smattering of polite applause.

Mr Finch presented the first piece to me, with all due ceremony. Other pieces soon circulated, until we had all been blessed with our own personal share of the stolen pineapple.

I eyed the yellow slice of fruit with some amount of scepticism.

"Well?" Mr Finch asked urgently. There was a pleading look on his face. I realised then that everyone else was waiting for me to take the first bite, as a matter of protocol.

I sighed—and shoved a tiny piece into my mouth.

The taste was... not what I had been expecting. In fact, it was like nothing I had ever tasted before in my life. It was somehow both sweet and tart at the same time. It numbed my mouth very slightly, in a way that I wasn't certain I liked.

I worked my mouth a few times, wincing in confusion.

"Er," I said finally. "That's... different, I suppose."

I wasn't strictly sure the fruit deserved its lofty price. But then... we hadn't really paid for it, had we?

The rest of the officers took my cue, digging into their pineapple with varying shades of eagerness and curiosity. Several strange expressions blossomed around the room.

I shot a careful glance at Mr Finch, as he chewed with great solemnity. He blinked slowly—and then, a look of pure, satisfied bliss dawned upon his pinched features.

"It's... every bit as good as I thought it would be," Mr Finch said reverently.

"It's *bizarre*," Lenore observed critically.

"What a strange texture," Holloway rumbled thoughtfully.

Evie blinked a few times. Just next to him, Little knitted his brow. *I'm not sure how I feel about it,* he signed.

"Right?" I said. "That's exactly it, I'm not sure at all."

Strahl watched the proceedings with an arched eyebrow. I imagined that he would have preferred to stand—but he had seated himself heavily into a chair, in a grudging concession to his injuries. One of his hands held Syrene carefully, where she leaned against his chair. The flowers atop her 'head' had changed overnight, into a wash of mauve foxglove blossoms. A subtle aura of peaceful bemusement radiated from her, infecting the rest of the room.

"You don't want a piece, Mr Strahl?" I asked him.

Strahl shook his head. "I've had pineapple before," he said. "It's terrible."

Mr Finch shot Strahl a sharp glance, as though the man had personally offended him. I decided it was time to move onto business, before someone started an argument about fruit.

I cleared my throat and stood up.

"As many of you are aware," I began, "Mr Strahl will be signing on with us. I have discussed the… *major*… rules with him. I trust that the rest of you will otherwise familiarise him with life aboard the *Rose*."

Strahl nodded stiltedly at the others around the table. Salutations echoed around the table from several quarters… but Dougal MacLeod remained conspicuously silent.

As the greetings died down, Dougal crossed his large arms over his chest.

"Ah dinnae see any fancy navigator, Mr Strahl," he said acidly. "Somethin' happen tae 'er?"

Strahl turned his gaze upon me, careful. "Will you give Syrene permission to introduce herself to the *Iron Rose*, Captain?" he asked me.

I wasn't quite certain what he meant by that—but I wasn't in the mood to argue particulars. "She has my permission," I said, with a hint of curiosity.

Gingerly, Strahl adjusted his grip upon the faerie, tapping her base against the deck.

Syrene *melted*.

Wood flowed like water, sinking down into the deck. Several of us stared incredulously, not quite certain what it was we were seeing. Dougal's scorn quickly turned to alarm; Lady Navi and Mr Finch shared a glance of sudden understanding. Evie blanched and reached for his husband's hand, while Lenore gripped at the pistol on her hip.

And then—the faerie was gone.

Strahl shot the room a wary look, before he spoke aloud: "Syrene," he said, "come out and say hello."

A new figure rose from the deck, stretching upwards like a sleepy yawn.

This time, Syrene looked… *somewhat* humanoid. She was taller even than Strahl—but impossibly slender. Graceful arms extended from that thin frame like sapling branches. The foxglove flowers I had noticed before crowned her head in a loose facsimile of cascading hair, framing an uncanny, expressionless face that reminded me of a wooden stage mask. Even as we watched, several spider-like eyes surfaced upon that face, gleaming like pieces of polished jet.

Silence fell, as Syrene tilted her head at the gathering.

Dougal stared, wide-eyed.

"Ah take it back," he whispered. "Ah don't wannae meet her anymore."

Navi bowed her head in reverence, as did Mr Finch—though I had the impression that he had averted his gaze partially out of fear. Lenore's expression went slack, and her hand fell away from her pistol—likely because she knew how little good a bullet would do her against a faerie.

Little, Evie, and I all shifted with instinctive shame. Syrene's presence heightened the discomforting awareness of our broken Oaths. More than ever, I felt the unworthiness of my broken honour. Tears threatened at Evie's eyes, and I knew that the feeling was especially magnified for him, as he wore the sash of the Benefactor. Holloway, too, had broken his Oath of service; he stared at the faerie with his one good eye, helplessly weary and full of despair.

Syrene's jet black eyes bore down upon me. Each one struck me like the business end of a separate rifle.

"We thank Captain Blair for his hospitality," Syrene intoned.

The faerie had no mouth. Nonetheless, the words echoed through the air, strange and mellifluous.

"We hereby swear to abide the captain's authority and follow his orders, so long as we remain upon his ship," Syrene added ponderously. "And... so long as such orders do not run counter to our greater duties."

The faerie's unblinking eyes rested patiently upon me. My mouth ran dry, in the resulting stillness. After a moment, I realised she was waiting for some sort of answer—so I forced a hurried nod.

Syrene continued, begrudgingly: "We further acknowledge that we owe our life and freedom to you, Captain Blair—and the life of our ward, as well."

She didn't look at Strahl as she said the words—but she didn't need to. Uncomfortable murmurs started up around the table. I tucked the knowledge into the back of my mind for a later date.

"We would see this debt repaid," Syrene said calmly. "However..." Her gaze drifted over me with displeasure—and then, it drifted further, over Evie, Little, and Holloway. "...we do not enjoy the company of Oathbreakers."

A frigid chill broke into her otherwise-pleasant voice. That tone raked across the four Oathbreakers in the room, sharp enough to draw blood.

Evie closed his eyes. *"For those who show mercy to others, my own mercy shall be as boundless as the sky,"* he whispered tremulously to himself. *"Therefore, learn forgiveness, and you shall be forgiven in turn."*

It was a prayer, I knew—a promise, straight from the Word of the Benefactor. Evie had sworn himself to the Benefactor, in an attempt to make up for the crimes of our youth. Now, as this creature of the Tuath Dé looked down upon us, he was praying that his service would suffice.

"That's easily fixed, isn't it?" Strahl interrupted pointedly. There was no holy fear in his voice as he addressed the faerie. His tone held only faint annoyance, and long familiarity.

Syrene turned her head to regard him.

Strahl shrugged. "I don't see anyone here who should be considered Oathbroken," he said. *"One* of us can remedy that."

I stared at him, dumbfounded by the implication.

There were rumours that certain faeries had the authority to forgive broken Oaths, under exceptional circumstances. Such a legendary boon was the sort of thing that only occurred in stories— and only after said faerie had assigned a terrible quest to the petitioner, in return for their redemption.

The forgiveness of the Tuath Dé was an invaluable treasure... more valuable, even, than pineapples.

Strahl stared down Syrene for a short eternity. I knew there was some unspoken conversation happening between them, but I was not privy to the details.

Finally, Syrene turned her featureless gaze back to the four of us.

The cobwebs of our shattered Oaths *shivered*, as though caught in an invisible breeze. I shivered too, as something unfamiliar touched upon my soul.

The sensation was abrupt; it disappeared almost as quickly as it had come.

Suddenly—entirely without fanfare—I was a whole man, once again.

Syrene's bitter disapproval eased into a strange, youthful delight. She tilted her head at me again, with an air of pleasure.

"We find this company to be far more acceptable," she said.

Evie looked up from his prayers, wide-eyed. Little's brown eyes filled with silent tears. The good physicker simply looked... stunned.

I wasn't certain how to feel. It didn't feel *real*. I wondered: shouldn't there have been more of a ceremony? After all of the shame and misery—after all of the years I'd borne Noble Gallant's displeasure—my redemption had come upon me like a sigh. It was an afterthought, really, granted for the sake of a faerie's annoyance.

Little reached out to embrace his husband, though, and I shoved the thought away. The rest of the crew looked on with thunderstruck expressions. Even Dougal seemed a bit caught up in the moment—and I knew for a fact that he had a less than religious view of the Tuath Dé and their servants.

William Blair, I told myself, *this is exactly what they call looking a gift-horse in the mouth.*

"Thank you," I said hoarsely. "Thank you. This is... a priceless gift."

Strahl looked away from me, strangely uncomfortable. I saw for a moment the same heavy guilt that Warden Ravenelle and I both carried with us. *Strahl never broke his Oath, whatever it was,* I thought. *He knows how fortunate he is.*

Silence stretched between us. Strahl seemed too conflicted to speak, and few other people wanted to be the first to draw Syrene's attention.

Trust Dougal MacLeod to save us from an awkward silence.

"So," he said, with exaggerated volume, "what's the next order ae business, Cap'n?"

I swallowed back the lump in my throat and straightened in my seat, looking around at my shell-shocked crew. "Next," I said, "we eat pineapple." I speared another cube of yellow fruit with my fork, in demonstration. "And *then*—we set a course for the Sirocco Isles."

Evie smiled and bowed his head to pray over our strange meal. "Blue skies and fair winds of fortune, my friends," he said.

I tucked into my last bit of fruit, trying not to think about the pale, nameless soldier, the faerie aboard my ship, and the spectre of a dead Imperium, following behind us.

Worst of all, however, was the creeping fear that I had begun to enjoy the taste of pineapple.

AFTERWORD

This hodge podge world of ours has been several years in the making.

William Blair's adventures started as a fun little exercise with our friends. We asked: what fantasy stereotypes would you like to see flipped on their heads? Mr Atwater started with the idea of a goblin hero, written seriously and not played for laughs. Someone else said "a happily married gay couple—and neither of them dies!"

The project expanded further and further, and friends continued making more and more heartfelt requests. Someone asked for an older female hero. Yet another person asked for a fantasy world where human people of colour didn't have to deal with racism. And it has been, quite honestly, an absolute joy to fulfil those requests. Each one made our world grow in ways we wouldn't have been able to imagine on our own.

We can't say that it's always been *simple* or *easy* to fulfil those requests. We're certainly not experts in every culture and every walk of life, and we've had to ask for a lot of help. But the learning process has been enjoyable—and however much work it has been, we wouldn't have it any other way. Our dearest hope is that whatever walk of life you tread, you can easily imagine yourself on the *Iron Rose*.

We have so many people to thank, even for this small novella.

Large thanks belongs to **Laura Elizabeth** and **Julie Golick** for their never-ending support and helpful editing. Thanks to **Ailbhe** for lending Dougal her Scottish accent, and to our many friends currently sweltering in Texas for Jasmine Albright's twang. Other thanks to **Vivekanand Ian Gurudata** for suggestions on Kumari Varma and the province of Aarushi and to **James Nettum** for contributions to Mr Samuel Méndez. Thanks also belongs to our sensitivity readers, who went to a lot of trouble explaining the underlying hows and whys of every issue so that we could learn from our mistakes. And lastly—*obviously*—we must thank every single member of the crew who contributed to this world. We hope you all enjoy your fantastical scoundrels and ne'er-do-wells.

THE ATWATER ADVENTURE COLUMN

In the mood for more swashbuckling adventures?
Join the Atwater Adventure Column to get writing updates, as well as
the exclusive novella *The Good, the Bad, and the Goblin*.

https://nicholasatwater.com/newsletter

ABOUT THE AUTHOR

Nicholas Atwater writes swashbuckling steampunk fantasy. He resides in Montreal, Quebec with his incredible, brilliant wife and two cats. As an ex-thespian, he certainly does not practice funny accents in the shower, and no one can prove otherwise. He is a veteran Dungeons & Dragons gamemaster, famously feared for both his villains and his puns.

* * *

In the mood for more swashbuckling adventures? Sign up for the Atwater Adventure Column. Subscribers also get early access to chapters from each book!

https://nicholasatwater.com
info@nicholasatwater.com